THE
MIDNIGHT
CURSE

THE MIDNIGHT CURSE

L.M. FALCONE

KCP FICTION

KCP Fiction is an imprint of Kids Can Press

Kids Can Press acknowledges the financial support of the Government of Ontario, through the Ontario Media Development Corporation's Ontario Book Initiative; the Ontario Arts Council; the Canada Council for the Arts; and the Government of Canada, through the BPIDP, for our publishing activity.

Published in Canada by	Published in the U.S. by
Kids Can Press Ltd.	Kids Can Press Ltd.
29 Birch Avenue	2250 Military Road
Toronto, ON M4V 1E2	Tonawanda, NY 14150

www.kidscanpress.com

Edited by Charis Wahl
Designed by Marie Bartholomew
Cover designed and illustrated by Céleste Gagnon

Printed and bound in Canada

This book is printed on acid-free paper that is 100% ancient-forest friendly (100% post-consumer recycled).

CM 10 0 9 8 7 6 5 4 3 2 1
CM PA 10 0 9 8 7 6 5 4 3 2 1

Library and Archives Canada Cataloguing in Publication

Falcone, L.M. (Lucy M.), 1951–
    The midnight curse / written by L.M. Falcone.

ISBN 978-1-55453-358-9 (bound). ISBN 978-1-55453-359-6 (pbk.)

I. Title.

PS8561.A574M54 2010   jC813'.6   C2009-903922-2

Kids Can Press is a *l'orus*™ Entertainment company

TO MY COUSIN, FRANK FALCONE,
WHO PLANTED THE SEED OF THE ITALIAN CHRISTMAS
CURSE THAT TURNED INTO THIS BOOK

TO TERRY KENNEDY — MY MUSE

TO THE DIVINE SPIRIT THAT MOVES
IN ME IN SUCH WONDROUS WAYS

THE MIDNIGHT CURSE

"Do you wish to have the curse removed or not?"
She spat out the words.

Charlie's hands shook as he put the cup to his lips. "It smells horrible!"

Mrs. Rothbottom wagged her finger at him. "It will work, I assure you. Though you may lose your sight for a few days."

"I'm gonna be blind?"

"Are you sure there isn't some other way?" I pleaded.

"It's the only way. So tell your brother to drink."

"Charlie. Just drink the darn thing!"

Charlie glared at me, plugged his nose and drank. Gasping like crazy, he finally got his voice back. "Is ... is the curse gone?"

1

"This isn't good," my brother, Charlie, kept saying. "Something bad's gonna happen. I can feel it in my bones — and my bones *never* lie."

Charlie and I are fraternal twins. That means we were born at the same time, but we're not at all alike. I'm cool, calm and sophisticated (yeah, right), with long red hair and sparkly brown eyes (when the light hits them just right). Charlie's a pain in the butt, a foot shorter than me and (because he never met a chocolate bar he didn't like) a foot wider.

Today's March 13, which just happens to be our birthday. It's also a Friday. Yup, Friday the Thirteenth. Charlie's the most superstitious kid you'll ever meet, and he was sure we were going to crash. We hadn't even taken off yet.

I ignored him and looked out the window, thinking back to the day before Spring Break. Everybody at school was bragging about where they were going for the holidays. Everybody but me. My mom doesn't have two nickels to rub together, so we weren't going anywhere. Every couple of years, when money gets really tight, Mom sells our living room furniture — every stick of it. The only thing she *didn't* sell this time was our TV. That's because Charlie threw himself on top of it and promised to do the dishes for the rest of his life. Mom took him up on the offer.

Sometimes, just when you think nothing's ever going to change in your miserable life, something happens. And that day it did. It came right out of the blue — a special-delivery letter from a dead relative.

"Jonathan Edward Darcy." Mom said his name really slowly. "He's your great-great-uncle on your father's side — the one no one talked about."

"Why not?" asked Charlie. "Was he retarded or something?"

Mom shot him a look. "Don't be rude."

"*What?* What'd I say?"

"He wasn't *retarded*, Charlie. He was a *recluse*. I remember Grandma telling me about how Uncle Jonathan refused to come to any family gatherings, never invited anybody to his place — wouldn't even *tell* anybody where he lived."

Mom looked over the letter. "Well, the mystery's finally solved. Uncle Jonathan lived in England — some place called Blaxston Manor in the village of Hampton Hollow."

"You gonna send flowers?" I asked, even though we didn't have the money.

"Too late. He died a month ago."

"No wonder they call it snail mail," sniffed Charlie.

"This isn't an invitation to the funeral," said Mom. "It's an invitation to the reading of the will."

"Did you say *will*?"

"I did indeed."

Charlie jumped right out of his chair. "*He left us money?*"

Mom wiggled her eyebrows and waved three plane tickets. "Pack your bags, kids. We're going to England!"

That's why we were sitting on a plane — three rows from the back — with Charlie so scared he looked like a ghost. Mom opened her purse and pulled out a crumpled picture. "Found this in an old album last night. It's your Uncle

Jonathan." The black-and-white picture showed a boy about fifteen years old wearing a long, shiny cape and holding a white rabbit.

"We have a magician in the family?" I asked.

Before Mom could answer, we heard a whirring sound from under the plane. Charlie gasped.

"It's just the luggage thingamajig," said Mom. "Calm down." She dug into her purse again and jammed a book into his hands.

"I don't wanna *read*," he whined.

"The lady at the gift shop promised me it would keep your mind occupied. Just give it a try."

The book was called *Brain Teasers* and it worked great. The more Charlie read, the calmer he got. But every couple of minutes he elbowed me. "Pick a number, Lacey. Any number. Any number at all."

"Two."

"Double it."

"Four."

"Add ten."

"Fourteen."

"Divide it in half."

"Seven."

"Take away your first number and what've you got?"

"Five."

Charlie held up his palm. He'd written the number five on it.

"How'd you do that?"

A voice came out of nowhere. "Ladies and gentlemen, this is Captain Besher. Departure will be a bit delayed as we're experiencing a minor technical difficulty with our —"

"We gotta get off!" Charlie raced up the aisle. Mom dragged him back, kicking and screaming. The "technical difficulty" turned out to be a landing-gear light that wouldn't shut off. No big deal. The steward put a damp cloth on Charlie's forehead, and fifteen minutes later we were in the air.

The first two hours of the flight passed okay.

Then ... things started to go wrong.

In the middle of lunch we hit turbulence. Everything flew up to the ceiling and came crashing down. Charlie got bonked on the head with his tray and smacked in the face with a fish.

Later, they showed a movie called *Terror in the Tunnel!* about a hijacked train full of orphans. Charlie's knuckles were white from gripping the armrest so hard, and he kept whining, "We're gonna die, Lacey. We're gonna die. I can feel it —"

"In your bones?"

He scrunched up his eyes and glared. "My bones *never* lie."

Charlie's always saying bad things come in threes. Well, I'm here to tell you, it's true.

When we finally got to England, there was this freak snowstorm and our plane had to circle the airport for a whole hour. Charlie was sure we'd run out of gas and started praying like crazy. He must've made the sign of the cross a hundred times — and we're not even Catholic.

When we landed, he threw himself on the ground and kissed it. "I'm never getting on a plane again — ever. Leave me here. I don't care. But I'm not going up again. Flying's for birds, not people. I'll walk home, thank you very much."

"Get in the darn taxi," snapped Mom, "or I'll kick you into tomorrow."

———

Snow pounded against the windows. The driver said, "Unusual weather for this time of year." I wondered how he could even see. Finally, he kicked the wipers on to high speed. They made scratching sounds, like nails on a blackboard. I plugged my ears so I wouldn't go totally bonkers, but then Charlie pulled a bag out of his coat pocket and stuck it under my nose. "Happy birthday, Lacey."

"I didn't get you anything."

"You gave me your 'I'm with Skanky' T-shirt last week."

"Not for your birthday."

"No big deal."

I looked inside: three mini Snickers bars.

"Wait a minute," I said. "You get ten for a buck. What'd you do with the other seven?"

"Ate 'em."

I whacked him with the bag.

Mom told us to relax and enjoy the scenery. What scenery? It was snowing so hard you'd think someone had thrown a blanket over the car.

To pass the time, Charlie read more brain teasers and I thought about all the new clothes I was going to buy once we got rich from Uncle Jonathan. Mom slept the whole way, her jaw hanging open like she was dead. Every once in a while she'd let out a rhinoceros snort that made Charlie and me jump.

"How'd Dad ever get any sleep with Mom snoring like that?"

Charlie's eyes got soft. "He loved her."

I caught the cab driver looking at us in the rearview mirror. "Your father's not on this trip?"

No matter how many times you say it, it never gets any easier. "Our father died. Four years ago. Car accident."

After what seemed like hours, we finally drove into a tiny village with houses and stores that looked really old-fashioned. It felt like we'd gone back in time a hundred years.

"This is Hampton Hollow."

The driver dropped us off at a tiny hotel with green shutters. After we checked in, we went down for supper. Charlie was thrilled when he spotted his favorite — baked beans in molasses — on the menu. He ate *three* bowlsful before Mom cut him off. She said he'd be tooting all night, and that's exactly what he did. His farting woke us up every five minutes. It sounded like we were in a war zone.

The next day the weather was still lousy, so we stayed inside watching TV until it was time to go to the reading of the will. At seven o'clock, we got dressed and went downstairs to get a taxi. We waited and waited. Charlie started worrying that if we were late we wouldn't get any money, but Mom said it didn't work like that. Finally, the taxi came and we all piled in. The driver headed out of the village, made a couple of turns, drove up a steep hill and went along a country road. After about five minutes, we bounced over a wooden bridge and stopped.

"Blaxston Manor," he said, in a voice that sounded way too much like Darth Vader's.

The manor stood alone in the middle of this huge field. It was three stories high with lots of arches and tall windows. Three gargoyles stared out into the darkness.

Charlie whispered, "Dracula would love this place."

2

The taxi turned up the driveway. Mom paid the driver and then the three of us climbed the stone steps up to the house. There had to be at least twenty of them. At the top, a nervous feeling came over me. I'm not sure why, exactly, but I think it had something to do with two old rocking chairs on the front porch. They were moving back and forth at the same time ... only nobody was in them.

Mom lifted a big brass knocker and banged it against the metal plate. The door slowly creaked open and an old man in a butler's uniform said, "Mrs. Darcy?"

"That's me."

"Please come in. We've been expecting you."

I couldn't believe how big the entrance hall was. "Our whole apartment could fit in here," I whispered to Charlie.

"I'll take your word for it." His glasses had fogged up.

"My name is Cornelius — Cornelius Twickenham. I worked for Mr. Darcy for forty-five
years."

Mom shook her head. "Such loyalty, Mr.
Twickenham!"

He smiled, and helped her with her coat. I
slid mine off, too.

"Will you allow me to take your coat and
scarf?" Cornelius asked Charlie. "It's quite warm
in here."

Charlie unwound his scarf and handed it over
with his coat. Cornelius hung everything on a
big coatrack shaped like a king's throne and
said, "If you'll kindly follow me, the lawyer's
waiting in the library."

The hallway we walked along was long and
dark. When we rounded the corner, Cornelius
suddenly stopped and looked at Charlie and
me. "These proceedings may take a while," he
said. "Why don't you and your brother explore
the house a bit? I'll take good care of your
mother."

Mom warned us not to break anything, or
she'd kill us. We promised, and headed back
down the hall.

The first room we came to had two huge
brown doors. They didn't open the regular way

but slid sideways right into the wall. We found ourselves in a gigantic living room totally covered with Christmas decorations.

Charlie grinned. "Christmas in March! I love it!" He looked around. "Maybe we'll get presents!"

"You wish."

Lights shimmered all over the place, and a tall decorated tree stood in the middle of the room. It was the most beautiful tree I'd ever seen — lit candles on every branch and a golden angel on top that looked like she was smiling right at me. Mom stopped putting up our little plastic Christmas tree after Dad died. She said it made her feel too sad.

As Charlie and I checked out the room, we spotted a huge tray of goodies — cakes, cookies and tons of chocolates.

"Do you think it's okay if we eat some?" I asked.

"Who'll know?" said Charlie, jamming a whole cookie into his mouth.

Everything tasted *so* good I could hardly stand it. Mom never had enough money to buy us treats like this.

A noise made me turn my head.

It was coming from the grandfather clock in the corner — a clicking sound, like the one when you're changing gears on a bike. Then it started bonging *really* loud.

Charlie jammed his fingers in his ears and I covered mine, but the bonging was so loud it hurt.

"Ow … Ow … Ow," Charlie cried.

"Come on!" I shouted.

We ran to the far end of the room and through a small black door. The bonging finally stopped, but our ears were still ringing. "I think my eardrums burst," Charlie muttered, hitting the side of his head with his hand. Sparkly stardust shot out of his ear.

I gasped and stepped back.

"What's in there, Lacey? *What?*"

I looked but couldn't see anything except earwax.

Charlie shook his head again, creating more stardust. "This is freakin' me out!"

I moved my hand. More sparkles appeared.

"It's not you, Charlie." I waved my hand really fast. "It's something in the air. See?"

We fooled with the stardust for a while and then walked around the room. It was filled with instruments — tubas, cellos, trumpets, drums. As we passed, each one did something. The tuba started playing all by itself and colorful bubbles floated out its bell. Then the cello opened like a door. When we leaned in to take a look, blue butterflies fluttered out and up to the ceiling.

The piano in the corner suddenly began to play.

We looked over and saw a man made of wood with his hands over the keys. His head slowly turned toward us. *"Name any song. I'll play it for you."*

Charlie called out, "'Ninety-nine Bottles of Beer on the Wall'" and, just like that, the wooden man played it. "Awesome."

We both sang along. When we got down to ninety-five bottles of beer, Charlie stopped. A funny look came over his fat face. "Uh-oh."

"What's wrong?"

"The *beans!*"

He took off like a shot.

I hung around singing more verses while Charlie went looking for a bathroom.

"Ninety-one bottles of beer on the wall, ninety-one bottles of beer. If one of the bottles should happen to fall, ninety bottles of beer on the wall."

The next thing I knew Charlie came racing back into the room through another door. His eyes bugged out when he saw where he was.

"How'd I get back *here*?"

I laughed and kept singing. *"Ninety bottles of beer on the wall, ninety bottles of beer. If one of the bottles should —"*

"Shut up!"

"— happen to fall, eighty-nine bottles of beer on the wall."

"I'm gonna burst! How can you just stand there singing?"

"It's easy. Watch. *Eighty-nine bottles of beer on the wall. Eighty-nine bottles of beer —"*

"I'm gonna get you for this, Lacey!"

"If one of those bottles should happen to fall …"

Charlie started crying. Just like a baby.

I rolled my eyes. "Okay. Okay. Stop bawling."

"Then help me!"

I followed Charlie out of the room and we ran around like crazy looking for a bathroom. Finally I found one and yelled, "Charlie! Over here!"

He flew inside. A second later he let out this humongous fart. It wasn't just loud but really, *really* long. I was so embarrassed I ducked into the next room.

There must've been at least a hundred mirrors in it. No matter where you stood, you could see your reflection over and over and over. I walked around, admiring myself from different angles, and then heard Charlie calling me. When I got back to the bathroom, the door was still closed.

"Charlie? Everything okay?"

No answer.

I knocked.

"Charlie?"

He still didn't answer, so I opened the door and stuck my head in. Charlie was gone — but the smell wasn't. I shut the door fast, then went looking for him.

I couldn't find him anywhere.

"Charlie … come out this minute!"

He didn't.

I knew Mom would kill me if I lost him. "Okay. You got me back. I'm sorry about the singing. Now, come out, come out, wherever you are."

Still nothing. I looked in every room and closet I could find. Charlie wasn't anywhere.

A bad feeling came over me. "Stop fooling around, you little creep. Where are you?"

When I got back to the front hall, I spotted a long, winding staircase. As I passed it I heard the steps above me creak.

I stopped, backed up … and smiled.

3

On the wall of the first landing I spotted a huge painting. It was a man dressed in a long, black jacket with a high collar. He was really old, with wavy white hair, a long nose and the saddest eyes I've ever seen. Had to be Uncle Jonathan.

Up the next flight I went, thinking for sure I'd see Charlie. I didn't. The top of these stairs brought me to the second floor.

There were fifteen doors — seven on the left, seven on the right and one at the very end of the hall. The one at the end was the only door that was a normal size. All the rest were huge.

"Charlie, you miserable maggot, where are you?"

Silence.

"Charlie!"

I tiptoed toward the nearest door across a deep red carpet with little yellow flower designs on it. Locked. The next one was open so I peeked in. It was a bedroom. White bedspread, white curtains, white furniture — even white roses. I knew it had to be my imagination, but I could swear the roses were humming. It soothed me and made me think of Mom. When Dad was still alive, Mom used to hum a lot around the apartment. He'd always say he knew she was happy when she hummed.

A shaft of moonlight suddenly came through the window. It made the roses sparkle. They were *so* beautiful I stepped inside and reached out to touch one. Just as I did, *all* the petals fell off. I scooped them up as fast as I could, jammed them into the vase and ran out.

I looked up and down the hallway. Nobody was there. Good. They'd never know I did it.

The next room I came to was a linen closet, and beside it was a bathroom. I wandered farther down the hall. The only sound was the creaking of the floor under my feet.

The next three rooms were all bedrooms, crammed with antique furniture.

"Charrrleee?"

At the far end of the hall was the smaller door.

I slowly opened it and poked my head inside. This room was round, with walls made of red brick. And it was empty ... totally empty.

A streak of white light flashed. Lightning? In winter?

The crack of thunder that followed shook the house so hard the windows burst open. I rushed over and pushed them shut.

Something moved in the yard.

Leaning my forehead against the cold glass I saw a big black tree. Through the falling snow I could make out a wooden swing dangling from ropes. It was going back and forth so fast it creeped me out.

As I started to leave, I noticed some stairs. They were made of the same red brick, so they blended right into the wall. A brass plate over the opening said **STAIRCASE 13**. I leaned in and whispered, "Charlie? You up there?"

I started climbing. At about the fifth or sixth step, I suddenly heard a really loud howling. Spinning around, I shot back down the stairs and lunged for the door. The knob wouldn't turn.

I jiggled it, but it wouldn't budge. I banged, but that didn't bring anybody. Neither did shouting.

There had to be another way out.

I ran back to the window. Maybe there was a ledge or fire escape. There wasn't. I heard the howling sound again.

But it was different this time. Then it hit me. *It's the wind. Just the wind.*

I relaxed a little, and tried the door again. When it still wouldn't open, I knew I had no choice. If I wanted to get out of there, I had to take the stairs.

Up I went, one step at a time. After about twenty steps, I spotted a door built right into the brick wall. The brass plate over it said STAIRCASE 9.

I opened the door a crack, then stuck my head through and saw a flight of wooden steps going down. There was a light at the bottom. I know this is going to sound nutty, but it felt as if the light was pulling me. I let it pull me, all the way down, step after creaky step. At the bottom, stretched out in front of me, was the longest hallway I'd ever seen. The walls and ceiling were the same red brick, but there were no doors and no windows. If I squinted I could just make out somebody at the far end.

"Hello?"

The person didn't answer.

"The door on the second floor locked on me!" I shouted. "Do you know another way out?"

Still no answer.

I started walking slowly along the hall. The farther I went, the colder it got — it reminded me of our apartment back home. I rubbed my arms. Where was the cold coming from? There was no opening anywhere.

When I got closer to the end of the hall, I could see that the figure was a boy sitting in a green rocking chair. He looked about my age. "Would you happen to know someone by the name of Charlie Darcy?" he asked.

"He's my brother."

The boy held up a bottle. "I've been asked to give this to him."

"Who asked you?"

"Jonathan Darcy … It's lovely, don't you think?"

"Yeah, but Charlie's not into bottles."

"Ahhh, but this is no ordinary bottle. This one has a *message* inside."

"What's the message?"

The boy smiled. "Haven't the foggiest. Apparently Jonathan whispered a message into it then corked it. When Charlie *uncorks* it, he gets to hear what it is."

"Neat." I took the bottle. "Do I get anything?"

"Not that I know of. Sorry."

The boy told me the only way back was up

Staircase 9. "The door sticks sometimes. Just give it a good kick."

Back I went, holding the bottle. When I got to the round room, I gave the door a hard kick and it flew open. Charlie was on the other side.

"Where've you *been*?" He sounded really mad. "I've looked all *over* the place. You know I hate being left alone. I'm telling Ma."

Before I could threaten him with an agonizing death, he spotted the bottle. "What's that?"

Thinking fast, I said, "Happy birthday, Charlie," and held it out to him.

"For me?"

Just as Charlie reached for it, I pulled it back. "*If* you don't tell Mom on me."

Charlie's eyes narrowed. "Keep the bottle," he said. "I wanna see you squirm when she kicks *you* into tomorrow." With that he turned and walked away.

"There's a message inside the bottle."

Charlie stopped. "What kind of message?"

"It's from Uncle Jonathan. That's all I know."

He slowly turned and walked toward me, holding out his hand.

"Do we have a deal?" I asked.

"Deal."

"Cross your heart and hope to die?"

"Yeah. Sure."

He quickly crossed his heart, and I handed him the bottle.

Charlie twisted the cork, yanked it with his teeth, wiggled it back and forth. But it wouldn't come out.

"How am I ever gonna get the message if the darn cork won't —"

"Let me try."

"Yeah, right. With your puny muscles?"

He put the bottle between his legs. One hard pull, and out popped the cork. Charlie grinned, shut one eye and looked inside the bottle. Then he held it up to his ear.

A deep, raspy voice whispered, "The midnight curse has been passed on to you!"

4

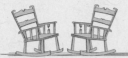

Charlie threw the bottle down. It smashed against the floor, shattering into a thousand pieces.

"What was that?" he screamed.

"I ... I don't *know*."

"What did he mean, *curse*? What did he mean, Lacey?"

"It's probably a joke." I tried to sound like it was no big deal. "You know. One of those gag gifts."

"Did you hear that voice? That's not a *joke* voice! I'm cursed! What am I gonna do? I'm *cursed*!"

"The kid!" I shouted.

"*What* kid?"

"The one who gave me the bottle. He'll know what's going on."

I ran back into the round room, bolted up the steps and yanked open the door in the wall. When I got to the bottom of those stairs, the hallway was empty.

Charlie came pounding behind me. "*Where is he?*"

"This doesn't make sense," I said. "There aren't any doors or windows. He couldn't just disappear."

"Magicians disappear all the time."

I ran down the hall.

"He isn't a magician."

"How do *you* know?"

"He was a *kid*, for crying out loud."

When I got to the far end, I ran my hands along the bricks and started pressing on them.

"What're you doing, Lacey?"

"If the only way back into the house is the way we came, he's gotta still be here."

"So where is he? I don't see any kid!"

"I don't *know*, Charlie. But he was sitting right here, in a green rocking chair! Maybe he's behind this wall."

"A hidden passage?"

"Well, it's possible."

We both felt around, trying to find a button or something, but there wasn't anything there.

"It's no use," cried Charlie, punching his fist against the bricks.

The wall swung open and he fell forward.

"*Lacey!*" His hand grabbed mine and pulled me inside.

Everything was pitch black.

"Where are we?" Charlie whimpered.

My heart was thumping hard. "I don't know."

A piano started playing far away.

I frowned. "D'you hear that?"

"I'm not deaf."

Suddenly the floor tilted and we shot down a long chute, screaming at the top of our lungs. A couple of seconds later we were spat out onto a hard floor.

"OWWW!"

I rolled over and sat up. "You okay, Charlie?"

He twisted his head. "I think I broke my neck."

As Charlie groped around for his glasses, I realized we were in a kid's playroom with model planes hanging from wires in the ceiling. In the middle of the floor was a castle surrounded by hundreds of toy soldiers, all marching together.

"I've been waiting for you."

A boy stepped through the castle gate.

"That's *him!*" I shouted.

Charlie slid his glasses on. "Who *are* you?"

"I'm the one who gave your sister the bottle."

"Well, I'm the one who *opened* it. And I don't want to be *cursed*. So take it back!"

"Afraid I can't."

Charlie lunged at him.

The boy moved and Charlie landed on top of some soldiers.

"Now, now. Violence will get you nowhere."

Charlie ran at him again.

"No, Charlie!"

I tried to stop him but both of us went crashing into the castle. My head hit something and everything went dark.

I don't know how long I was out for, but as my eyelids slowly lifted I could feel my head hurting.

The door opened and Cornelius walked over to me, carrying a silver tray with a glass on it. "Would you care for some orange juice?" he asked. "Freshly squeezed."

"Where am I?"

"Why, in your bedroom, of course."

My eyes shot around. I was in the room with the white roses.

"This *isn't* my bedroom."

"Are you sure?"

"Of course I'm sure!"

"I'll take the juice," said a voice.

I spun around and saw the same boy, sitting in a chair by the window. Cornelius walked over and handed him the juice. Then he nodded and left.

"Who are you? What'd you do with Charlie? Where's my mom?"

"My name is Daniel. I've kidnapped Charlie. Your mother is dead."

"Lacey!" A hand smacked my face.

"Ow!" My eyes popped open and I saw Charlie staring at me.

"Are you okay?"

I sat up quickly and looked over at the chair. It was empty. "Where'd he go?"

"Where'd who go?"

"*Daniel.*"

"Daniel who?"

"He said he kidnapped you and that Mom was dead!"

"*Dead?*"

I spotted the blue bottle on the dresser. "How can it still be here? You smashed it."

"Smashed what?" asked Charlie.

"Don't you remember? The curse!"

"*What* curse?"

"'*The midnight curse has been passed on to you.*'"

Charlie's eyes bugged out and he raced into the hall. I leaped out of bed and chased him. We practically flew down the stairs, the whole time Charlie screaming, "Help! Help! Somebody help!"

Daniel stepped right in front of him. "Is something wrong?" He took a bite of a sandwich.

Charlie ran behind him, then pointed over Daniel's shoulder at me. "My sister's gone *crazy*, that's what's wrong."

"Oh." Daniel took another bite. "This definitely needs pickles."

He went back down the hall.

Charlie and I stared at each other. I took a step forward. He took a step back.

"I'm not crazy, Charlie. Something strange is going on in this house."

"What d'ya mean, strange?"

"Don't you remember the bottle?"

"*What* bottle?"

"The one Uncle Jonathan gave you."

Charlie's eyes darted around, looking for a way out. "Uncle Jonathan's *dead*. How could he give me a bottle?"

"Wait here. Don't move."

"Sure. No problem."

"*Promise* me."

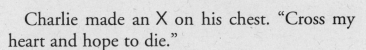

Charlie made an X on his chest. "Cross my heart and hope to die."

I bolted back up the stairs. When I ran into the bedroom, the bottle was still there. Good. Then I spotted a tiger design etched into the glass.

Different bottle.

5

When I got back downstairs, Charlie was gone. Pickles!

I ran to the back of the house, down a short flight of stairs, around a corner and into the dining room. As I moved through it I heard, "D-o y-o-u t-h-i-n-k i-t w-i-l-l w-o-r-k?"

It sounded like a kid's voice talking really slowly.

Then Daniel said, "I'll do everything in my power to make it work."

When I stepped into the kitchen, Daniel was standing beside the fridge holding a jar with one hand and sliding out a long, flat pickle with the other. No one else was there.

"Who were you talking to?" I asked, moving closer to him.

"No one."

"I heard somebody."

Daniel looked at me and smiled. "I talk to myself occasionally. It passes the time."

What was he trying to pull? "That other voice *wasn't* yours."

"Hearing voices now, are we? Perhaps Charlie's right. You are crazy."

I felt my face flush. "I'm not crazy and you know it."

"All I know is I love pickles." He held out the jar. "Would you care for one?"

I grabbed the jar and threw it in the garbage bin. Then I stared straight into his eyes. "You *gave* me a bottle."

"Did I?"

"The bottle had a *curse* in it."

He looked surprised. "A what?"

"You know it. I know it. And you're not leaving this room until you tell me what's going on."

"Whatever are you talking about?"

I raised my fist to punch him.

"T-e-l-l h-e-r."

I gasped and spun around.

"T-e-l-l h-e-r."

Daniel hissed, "Go back to your chair."

"Who are you talking to?"

He didn't answer.

The only place anybody could hide was under the table. As I bent down to look, a shadow fell over me.

"Hey, Lacey."

Charlie walked straight to the refrigerator and swung open the door. "Cornelius said there's pizza in here — pepperoni and mushroom."

"Heating it up will improve the taste." Daniel pointed to the toaster oven.

Charlie slid in a couple of slices, then slammed the door and turned the knob. "You gotta see the game room they've got here, Lace. It's *awesome*."

"Go on," said Daniel. "I'll deliver the pizza when it's ready."

Charlie pulled me out of the room. When we got to the door, I stopped and looked back. Daniel mouthed, "Later."

Charlie led me to the front hall and down a flight of stairs — **STAIRCASE 7**. We came out into a gigantic arcade with flashing lights, pinball machines, a basketball court, a mini-golf course and cars with television screens for windshields. It really *was* awesome.

Charlie grabbed a basketball, bounced it a couple of times and shot it at a hoop. It went straight in. He gave a loud whoop, then jumped behind the wheel of a sports car. As he turned the ignition key, the windshield came to life and he started driving. The road on the screen flew at him, but no matter what popped up, Charlie swerved, missed it and stayed on the road. His points made loud ringing sounds as they racked up.

I walked around a bit and spotted Cornelius standing behind a popcorn machine wearing a red-and-white-striped apron. He scooped up a huge bag of popcorn and pumped hot butter over the top.

Suddenly, the room turned ice cold.

A voice whispered in my ear. "M-a-k-e h-i-m t-e-l-l y-o-u."

I swung around.

No one was there.

Daniel came down the stairs holding the pizza and walked it over to Charlie. Charlie didn't even look at him — just reached out, grabbed a slice and kept driving with his other hand.

I was so scared my body was shaking. Daniel must've seen how desperate I was because in a soft voice he said, "Come back up, Lacey."

When we got to the first floor, he told me to wait. A minute later he came back holding a picture in a silver frame. Motioning for me to follow him, he led me toward the front door and outside.

It had stopped snowing.

Daniel sat on the top step and patted the spot next to him. I sat down.

"Some people can't be hypnotized," he said. "You're one of them, Lacey."

"You tried to *hypnotize* me?"

"It didn't work. As I said, some people —"

"Why would you want to hypnotize me?"

"To protect you."

"From *what*?"

"The truth."

"The truth. What truth? About the bottle?"

Daniel's eyes held mine for a long moment. "Yes. Your brother thinks you've gone crazy, but *he's* the one who's going to go crazy. That's the reason I hypnotized him — so he'd stay calm until the last moment."

"There *is* a curse, isn't there!"

Daniel slowly nodded.

6

It felt like somebody'd punched me in the stomach. "Tell me what the curse is."

He shook his head. "It's best if you wait along with Charlie."

"Wait for *what*?"

"Midnight. Three claps and he'll snap out of the hypnotic state. Then I'll tell you both."

"Why does he have to wait till midnight?"

"If I tell him now, he'll go crazy. But if I tell him just before midnight, he'll be too busy … trying to stay alive."

My eyes opened wide. "Tell me what the curse is."

"Not yet."

"*Tell* me."

"You're *sure* you want to know, Lacey?"

I was scared, but I had to know. I nodded. Daniel turned the picture over. "This is your great-great-uncle Jonathan on his twenty-fifth birthday." He handed me the picture. "And

43

that beautiful woman beside him is Catherine Manridge."

The picture was cracked and yellowish. In it Uncle Jonathan was smiling, but Catherine had a faraway look in her eyes.

"Your uncle fell deeply in love with Catherine but, alas, her heart belonged to his best friend, Robert Collins. Jonathan became insanely jealous — so jealous that when Robert asked Catherine to marry him, your uncle plotted to stop the wedding."

"Stop it how?"

"Robert was an apothecary, and he made potions to help people when they got sick. The potions worked well, for the most part, but one day a young girl died only hours after Robert had given her a potion to cure her dizzy spells. The girl's father blamed him, and everyone believed he was guilty."

"Just because the girl's father accused him?"

Daniel shook his head. "Because of Jonathan. He told the police that he saw Robert put mandrake into the potion."

"What's mandrake?"

"A poisonous root." Daniel leaned forward. "Robert was arrested, found guilty and sentenced to hang."

"That's awful."

"It gets worse. While he was in jail, Robert asked for Jonathan to come and see him. But Jonathan was too much of a coward. In three long months, he never went to visit — not once.

"Finally, on a snowy March day, Robert was taken to the gallows. As he stood on the platform he spotted Jonathan. But Jonathan's head was down.

"Robert said, 'Look at me.'

"Jonathan couldn't. How do you look into the eyes of a friend you've betrayed?

"As they put the rope around his neck, Robert shouted his innocence. But no one believed him.

"Robert knew the truth. He knew that your uncle had betrayed him, and he hated him for it. Hated him so much that" — Daniel stared off into the distance — "as they put the rope around his neck, he put a curse on Jonathan."

"The midnight curse?"

"*Every night of your life, until you have the courage to face me, you must sleep in water or you shall shrivel up and die.*"

"What kind of curse is that!?"

"It's called a torture curse — one that goes on and on. Robert wanted revenge, and this curse assured that your uncle would never marry Catherine, *and* that he'd suffer his whole life."

I couldn't believe what I was hearing.

"Then Robert said, 'If you die *before* you face me, the midnight curse shall pass on to the next male in your family.'"

"Charlie?"

"Actually, your great-grandfather, your grand-father and your father were the next males. But all three are dead."

"In all these years no other boys were born?"

"Only girls — until your mother had Charlie. I can show you your family tree, if you wish."

"Wait a minute. Your story doesn't make sense. How could Uncle Jonathan face Robert if Robert had been hanged?"

"Robert's *body* died that day," said Daniel, "but his *spirit* attached to your uncle and came home with him. Every time your uncle moved, the spirit moved with him. For years he's lived in Blaxston Manor."

"Here?"

Daniel nodded. "In the attic." His eyes got dark. "And as each year passes, Robert's spirit grows angrier."

"Why didn't Uncle Jonathan just go up and apologize? That would have ended it!"

"Lacey, he *tried*. But his terror was always too great. This final time, he got as far as stepping *inside* the attic."

I swallowed hard. "And?"

"He had a heart attack."

"Is … is that how he died?"

Daniel handed me the picture and slowly stood up. He walked over to the first chair, sat down and began rocking back and forth. The other chair started rocking, and the ghostly figure of a boy appeared sitting in it.

My heart thumped in my chest so hard I thought it'd break through.

"That's how we all died," said Daniel, staring straight ahead.

Then both of them disappeared.

7

I screamed like a crazy person, raced back into the house, slammed the door and locked it. Then I ran downstairs. When I grabbed Charlie, his hands slipped off the steering wheel and the car he was driving crashed.

"Aw, maaaan!"

"Come on!" I shouted.

"I had eighty-five thousand points!"

I looked over at the stairs. "We gotta get out of here!"

"*Why?*"

"I'll explain later."

He pulled away. "Explain *now*."

I dragged him out of the seat and shoved him over to the stairs. When we got to the top I poked my head through the door. No Daniel. Good.

"Tell me what's wrong," whined Charlie.

"We have to leave."

"But I *like* it here."

"You won't like it if we stay."

"What're you talking about?" He headed back down the stairs.

I grabbed his sweater.

"Lacey!"

I pulled him up and pushed him into the hallway. Then I grabbed our coats off the wooden rack and threw Charlie's at him.

"Where's Mom? We can't go without Mom."

"She already left," I lied.

"That's not possible. She wouldn't leave without us."

"The reading of the will was in the village. At an office."

Charlie shook his head. "No way Mom would go without telling us."

"She told *me*."

"*When?* When did she tell you?"

I had to think fast. "When you were in the bathroom. The beans? Remember?"

Cornelius came walking toward us. "Is anything wrong?"

"Did Mom really leave?" Charlie asked.

Cornelius looked at me, then at Charlie. "She was taken to the solicitor's office for the reading of Mr. Darcy's will."

Why was he backing up my story?

"Do you think they're finished yet?" I wondered if he'd keep the lie going.

"I was just informed that they are ready to leave. My instructions are to take you there. It's not far."

"Good."

"Can't we stay a little longer, Lacey?"

"No, we can't! Now let's go."

"But I really *like* it here."

Why was he being so stubborn? Then I remembered: he was still hypnotized.

"Don't you want to find out how much Uncle Jonathan left us?"

Charlie's eyes lit up. "Oh yeah! The *money*."

"I'll bring the car around," said Cornelius.

"We're coming with you." No way was I going out the front door with two ghosts on the porch.

"Of course," said Cornelius.

Charlie and I stayed right behind him as he led the way to the back of the manor. When we stepped outside, Charlie shivered. "Man, it's cold." He buttoned his coat.

An old-fashioned car, like the ones in black-and-white gangster movies, was parked close to the door.

I jumped into the backseat. "Come *on*, Charlie."

He slid in beside me. "What's the big hurry?"

Cornelius started the engine and snapped on the headlights. They shone through the dark onto the swing hanging from the tree branch. There was no wind, but the swing was still moving.

I waited for Cornelius to get going. He didn't. Instead he rummaged around in the glove compartment. What was he doing? Why wasn't he going?

My heart started pounding, but I fought to keep my voice calm. "Um … what's wrong, Cornelius?"

"I'm afraid I've misplaced my glasses. Can't drive without them." He slowly turned to us. "I'll only be a moment."

He walked back to the house.

"My *scarf*," said Charlie. "I forgot it, too."

He reached for the door handle. I yanked him back. "You can get it next time."

"But it's *freezing*."

He reached out again. I yanked him back even harder.

"Don't go, Charlie. *Please*."

"Why not? Why are you acting so crazy?"

"I can't explain right now! Just trust me! *Okay?*"

"All right. All right. Sheesh."

We waited for Cornelius to come back.

He didn't.

Something was wrong.

Maybe the ghosts got him. Maybe …

Just then Cornelius came out wearing his glasses. I said a silent thank-you and breathed a huge sigh of relief — until the car door swung open.

"There's been a change of plans. Mr. Darcy's solicitor called to say that he and your mother are returning here for a late dinner. Come along."

I held on to Charlie's coat as he started to get out.

"What're you doing, Lacey? Let *go*."

Cornelius turned around. "Is there a problem?"

I smiled. "No. No problem."

He smiled back and went inside.

"Close the door, Charlie. I have something to tell you."

Charlie *finally* clued in that I was serious. He closed the door.

I clapped my hands three times.

8

"*Cursed!?*" Charlie screamed. "What did he mean, Lacey?"

When he realized he was inside a car, he shouted even louder. *"How'd we get here?"* He looked in his hands. *"Where's the bottle?"*

"That's not important."

Charlie totally freaked. *"WHAT'S GONNA HAPPEN TO ME?"*

I grabbed him. "I won't let anything happen to you! I *promise.*"

He pushed me away. "What can *you* do? You can't do anything! *I'm the one who got cursed!*"

"Calm down, Charlie! *Please.*"

Daniel was right. I shouldn't have told him until the last minute.

Then I noticed the car keys. Cornelius hadn't taken them!

I yanked Charlie out of the back seat, opened the driver's door and shoved him in.

"*What're you doing?*"

"You're gonna drive."

I ran around to the front and got in beside him.

"I can't drive!"

"You drove in the arcade. You got eighty-five thousand points. You're a *great* driver."

"Lacey! Are you crazy?"

"Just put it in drive, Charlie, and *go*."

"*I can't!*"

I grabbed his face and twisted it toward me. "Listen! This isn't a joke. You've *got* to get us out of here. You're the only one who can do it. Start driving, Charlie! *Pleeease?* Start driving!"

A change came over him, like he really understood how serious this was. He straightened his glasses, put the car into drive and pounded the gas pedal. We shot forward. He slammed on the brake with both feet.

"Easy, Charlie!"

A loud knock on the window made us jump. Cornelius flung open the door. I slammed it hard and screamed, "GO, CHARLIE! GO!!"

Charlie jammed his foot on the pedal and took off. He was so scared he drove the car right into the field, heading straight for some trees.

"Look out!"

Charlie spun the steering wheel. The car scraped against a trunk, bark flying everywhere. Then we crashed through a wooden fence and bounced like crazy over a dried-up garden.

Charlie turned the wheel again and we went in a big circle.

Daniel was standing right in front of us! Charlie screamed as he drove straight through him.

"Where'd he come from?"

"Keep driving!"

"Did I *kill* him!?"

"No! Keep driving!"

Cornelius was waving and shouting, "Stop! Stop!"

But we didn't.

Charlie drove around the manor and down the driveway. He didn't even brake when he got to the road, just turned really hard and headed for the bridge. The wooden planks clunked as we sped over them.

Charlie stared straight ahead. The car swerved a lot, but it stayed on the road. When we'd gotten pretty far away, he pulled over and jerked to a stop.

Neither of us said anything for a long time.

"I'm sorry, Charlie. It's my fault. If I hadn't —"

"What's ... the ... curse?"

"It's better if you wait to hear it."

Charlie slowly turned his head. "What ... is ... it?"

I shook my head. "You'll worry too much if I tell you now."

"*Tell* me."

I knew he wasn't going to let up until I told him. I swallowed hard and said, "You ... you have to sleep in water. Every night of your life. Or you'll shrivel up and die."

Charlie's eyes got huge. *"Whhhaat?"*

"I'm sorry. I'm *sorry*. The curse was put on Uncle Jonathan a long time ago. See, he betrayed his best friend, so when his friend died he cursed Uncle Jonathan so that he'd suffer his whole life."

Something told me not to tell Charlie the part about having to face the spirit in the attic. He was scared enough.

"Uncle Jonathan's *dead!*" he yelled.

"Yes, but ... there's another part."

"Aw, man."

"If Uncle Jonathan dies, the curse passes to the next male in the Darcy family."

"Me! *I'm* the next male?"

"I'm sorry."

"Stop saying you're sorry!"

I touched Charlie's arm. He pulled away.

"This doesn't make sense. Who puts a curse in a bottle? Why *do* that?"

A voice behind us said, "So you'd know what was happening."

Charlie and I swung around. Daniel was in the backseat.

9

Charlie's eyes were wild. "It's him! The boy I hit!"
Daniel shrugged. "Didn't hurt a bit."

"How'd *you* get in here?" I shouted.

"When Charlie drove through me I remained in the car."

"Pleeease go away," Charlie begged.

"I'm afraid I can't."

Charlie was shaking like a leaf. "W-w-who are you?"

"I'm a boy."

"Y-y-you're a *ghost*."

"That, too. Yes. I'm definitely a ghost."

Charlie whimpered.

"There are two of us."

"*Two* ghosts?" Charlie's eyes rolled back in his head and he passed out cold.

"Matty and I are stuck at the manor." Daniel kept talking like nothing had happened.

I slapped Charlie's cheek. "What do you mean, stuck?"

"When Matty and I broke in, we died so traumatically that our spirits went into a sort of emotional shock. Now we're stuck. Can't go back to our old life, can't move on."

"Why'd you break into the manor?"

"To steal the treasure."

Charlie instantly came to. *"Treasure?"*

"Welcome back." Daniel smiled.

"What treasure?" Charlie sounded interested.

"For years everyone talked about Blaxston Manor, telling stories about a treasure in the attic. They said that Mr. Darcy never went out at night because he was protecting it. Matty and I — we didn't have any family — scrounged around for food wherever we could get it. And Mr. Darcy had the treasure all to himself. It didn't seem fair. So one morning we waited for him and Cornelius to leave, then broke in."

Charlie pushed his glasses up his nose. "Did you find it?"

"No," said Daniel. "When we entered the attic, both Matty and I died of fright."

"What'd you see?" we asked at the same time.

"Nothing."

I frowned. "What'd you mean, nothing? You can't die from *nothing*."

"Who cares what he saw," cried Charlie. "We

gotta do something about the curse!"

"You're right, Charlie," said Daniel. "And I'm going to help you."

"*How?* How are you gonna help me?"

"All we have to do is lift the curse. Then the evil spirit will go away."

Charlie's voice and eyebrows shot up. *"Evil spirit?"*

Daniel clapped his hands three times and Charlie froze. "You will forget that I ever mentioned an evil spirit." Daniel turned to me. "I assumed you'd told him."

"He was already too scared."

"A wise move."

Charlie was staring straight ahead like a zombie.

"Matty and I wish to live in peace at the manor," said Daniel. "We have a good life there. Jonathan and Cornelius have given us everything — toys, games, the arcade and all the food we can eat."

"Ghosts can't eat."

"That's what I believed, as well. However, for some reason we can. Everything Cornelius cooks tastes wonderful. He makes anything we desire. It's a good life." He slouched a bit. "Except for the evil spirit."

"Shhh!"

"Charlie can't hear us, Lacey."

"Are you sure?"

"Positive."

I relaxed a little. "I thought the way to get rid of the curse was by facing the spirit."

"That's precisely what Robert thought. But I'm sure there are other ways. I've been doing quite a bit of reading about curse removals and the like."

And the like? Daniel sure didn't sound like a normal kid.

"Wouldn't it be a whole lot easier if Charlie just *faced* the spirit?"

"Of course. But if he goes into the attic, he'll likely die of fright, just as we did. Then we'll all be stuck with Robert's spirit until the next Darcy male comes along."

Daniel clapped his hands three times and Charlie snapped out of his trance. "I'm going to help you get rid of the curse, Charlie."

"Really?"

"Really. But first, we need a psychic."

Charlie looked confused. "What's a psychic?"

"Think fortune-teller, only more powerful."

"And just where are we going to find a psychic?" I asked.

"Right here. Mrs. Rothbottom's good. Strange, but good. She helped many people in my day." He looked at Charlie. "Just drive through the village to Willow Lane."

Charlie started the car. Since it was dark, we didn't worry about anybody seeing that a kid was driving.

"Willow Lane's coming up on the right," said Daniel.

Charlie slowed down and I leaned forward to see better. "There it is." I pointed. "Just after that fence."

"If I remember correctly," said Daniel, "Mrs. Rothbottom lives in the second cottage on the left."

Charlie glanced over his shoulder. "Do you really think she can help me?"

"Of course she can." Daniel sounded absolutely sure. But I wasn't.

In less than a minute we were at the cottage. Charlie shut off the engine.

"Good luck," said Daniel.

"You're not coming in with us?"

He shook his head. "Not possible."

"Why *not*?" Charlie sounded desperate.

"My energy is bound to the manor, the grounds

and the things thereof. That includes this car. I'm unable to leave it."

The cottage was set pretty far back from the road. I could see a lamp over the door that cast a circle of light on the front steps, but every window was dark. "I don't think she's home."

"Good." Charlie started the car.

The key turned off by itself and the doors sprang open.

Daniel nodded toward the cottage. "There's only one way to find out."

"Aw, man."

Charlie and I got out of the car and slowly started up the stone path. I looked back at Daniel. He gave me a little smile.

We got more and more nervous as we neared the house. Suddenly, a horrible shriek cut through the air.

Charlie screamed as two black cats jumped out of the bushes, shot in front of us and disappeared around the side of the cottage.

"It's okay. It's okay." My heart was pounding. "It's just cats."

"*Black* cats," cried Charlie. "*Both* of them! *Two* black cats! Double bad luck!"

"They're just cats. Who cares what color they are?"

"It's a warning. Let's get outta here." He headed back to the car.

I ran after him and spun him around. He slapped me away. "Leave me alone, Lacey! I wanna go back to the hotel!"

"We can't go there now!"

"Why not? Why can't we? When Mom sees we aren't at the manor, she'll go there. For sure. She's probably waiting for us."

"No, she's not!"

"How do *you* know? You don't know anything!"

I had to tell him.

"Charlie ... Mom never left the manor."

"What are you talking about?"

"I lied so that you'd leave with me."

"But Cornelius said —"

"He lied, too."

"Why would he lie? *Why?*"

"I haven't figured that out yet. But he's up to something. I can feel it —"

"In your bones?"

I smiled. "In my bones."

"Bones never lie, Lacey."

The car horn gave a honk and we both looked over. Daniel waved us toward the cottage.

In that moment I knew one thing: there was no going back.

"Look, Charlie. Maybe Mrs. Rothbottom can help you, maybe she can't. But we're here now, so let's give it a try."

Even though he was scared, Charlie nodded. Then he did something he hadn't done since we were little — he slipped his hand into mine. We walked up to the cottage together.

10

Charlie and I stood in front of a dark green wooden door. Just as I reached up to knock, it swung open. We both gasped.

A tall lady with big blue eyes and dark frizzy hair stood looking down at us. Her eyes narrowed as she looked back and forth between us.

"Ah, curses," she said, shaking her head. "Nasty business."

"How did you know?" Charlie cried.

"Come in. It's cold."

As we stepped inside I noticed a small sign on the wall written in fancy letters.

Spell for money £30
Spell for love £55
Spell for health £45
Jinxes lifted £35
Curses removed £40

Mrs. Rothbottom took us into the living room and motioned for us to sit on the couch beside the fireplace. The flames made loud crackling sounds as I told her who we were and about how Uncle Jonathan had been in love with Catherine Manridge.

"There was a Catherine Manridge who lived here in the village," she said. "Years ago now. It's not a common name."

I explained about Robert being hanged after Uncle Jonathan lied, and the curse Robert put on him, and how it got passed on to Charlie.

When I finished, Mrs. Rothbottom turned to him. "Hmm. I wonder if you're really cursed."

Charlie's jaw dropped. "You mean … maybe I'm *not*?"

"It's a distinct possibility. Many people use the power of the mind against their enemies. If people *believe* they've been cursed, they often bring evil upon themselves." She stood up and straightened her skirt. "I must first determine if a curse truly has been cast."

"How are you gonna do that?"

"Follow me."

Mrs. Rothbottom led us through the kitchen and down a flight of rickety old stairs. When we got to the bottom she snapped on a lightbulb dangling from the ceiling. The room had no windows, and the only furniture was a table and chair tucked in the corner and a black chair in the middle with a circle of candles around it.

Mrs. Rothbottom told Charlie to step over the candles and sit in the chair.

I whispered, "Go on."

Mrs. Rothbottom motioned for me to sit at the table and told me not to make a sound. Then she switched off the light.

Everything went black.

"Close your eyes, Charlie," Mrs. Rothbottom said. "Breathe deeply and let the air flow out very slowly. Do this seven times, if you please."

As Charlie breathed, Mrs. Rothbottom struck a match and lit a long, thin stick with it. She used the stick to light the first candle.

In a soft voice she said, "Picture yourself surrounded by white light." She moved to the next candle. "With each breath, feel all your worries floating away." She continued slowly around the circle. "Relax deeply, Charlie. Very ... very ... deeply."

When she'd lit all the candles she put the tip of the stick into a small pot. I heard a hissing sound, and a curl of smoke drifted up. She leaned the stick against the wall, then walked over to a cabinet I hadn't noticed before.

Mrs. Rothbottom opened the cabinet and I saw a diamond-shaped mirror hanging inside it. She gently lifted the mirror and held it in front of her, the glass facing out. She walked around the circle of candles three times, then hung the mirror on the wall facing Charlie.

"Slowly open your eyes," she said.

Charlie opened his eyes.

"I'm going to ask you to blink one hundred times. On the hundredth blink, if you are truly cursed, you will see a vision. If you are *not* cursed, the mirror will reflect only you." Charlie stared straight ahead. "You may start now."

Charlie began blinking. I counted each blink inside my head. It seemed to take forever but he finally reached ninety. That's when I started praying really hard that he'd be okay.

Ninety-three ... ninety-four ... ninety-five ... ninety-six ... ninety-seven ... ninety-eight ... ninety-nine ...

A white mist swirled around the surface of the mirror. My stomach tightened. The mist disappeared and the mirror showed Charlie floating face-up in a pool of water, his arms outstretched.

"You're cursed," said Mrs. Rothbottom.

11

Charlie burst out crying.

"Stop it," snapped Mrs. Rothbottom.

He didn't.

"Crying will do you no good. Stop it this instant."

"I can't!"

"You're frightened and you'd be a fool *not* to be. However, all the tears in the world will not solve your problem."

Mrs. Rothbottom grabbed the long stick and attached something to the end of it, then used it to snuff out the candles. The room was dark again.

"Lacey?" Charlie's voice shook.

I stood up quickly. "I'm here, Charlie."

The lightbulb snapped back on.

I looked over at Mrs. Rothbottom. "Now what do we do?"

"We counteract the curse, of course." She turned

and climbed back upstairs. "Time for tea."

I moved over to Charlie and pulled his sleeve. "Come on."

"But I don't like tea."

I smacked him.

At the stove, Mrs. Rothbottom was throwing things into a bowl and muttering to herself. "Vetivert, galangel, wintergreen, a pinch of salt, a dash of pepper and" — she stuck her hand deep into a brown jar — "eight chicken feathers."

Charlie eyeballed me. "*Chicken* feathers?"

The feathers went in and then Mrs. Rothbottom poured a yellow liquid over the whole mess.

Suddenly, the flame on the burner shot up. I didn't even see her turn it on.

She lifted a metal teapot from a shelf, poured everything into it and set it on the burner.

"Now" — she turned to Charlie — "we must do a cleansing."

"A cleansing?"

"Yes."

"Will it hurt?"

She smiled. "Not a bit." With her big eyes and crooked teeth, she looked like a crazy person. "Outside we go."

As we moved over to the door I asked, "Why outside?"

"This type of cleansing is most powerful by the light of a full moon, and tonight the moon is definitely full." She put her hand on Charlie's shoulder. "Have you any idea how lucky you are?"

"Lucky? I've been *cursed.*"

"There are worse things."

"Oh, yeah? Name one."

"You could have been married to *Mr.* Rothbottom, rest his soul." She laughed and picked up two thick white candles.

As we followed her outside, Charlie whispered, "Do you think she knows what she's doing?"

"Of course she does." I tried to sound confident, like Daniel.

As we crunched through the snow in the back-yard I thought of Daniel, and wondered if he was getting tired waiting for us. But then I figured ghosts probably don't get tired.

The moon was huge.

Mrs. Rothbottom stopped under a tall, skinny tree with thousands of dried leaves still on it. All the branches were pointing up. It looked like they were praying.

She put one candle on an iron stand, walked around the tree and put the other one on a second stand. Then she lit them both.

"Come here, luv," she said to Charlie, "and stand facing the trunk." Her voice sounded different outside. Softer. Kinder.

Charlie moved closer to her. "What're you gonna do?"

"Be quiet."

"Okay."

Mrs. Rothbottom turned to me. "Go inside, Lacey, and check the tea. If it's boiling, turn off the stove and bring me the pot. Be careful not to burn yourself."

I crunched back through the snow.

Inside the kitchen, steam was pouring out of the teapot. It was definitely boiling.

I grabbed the handle.

"OUCH!"

My hand hurt like crazy, so I ran to the sink, turned on the cold water and stuck my fingers under it. How could I be so dumb?

Mrs. Rothbottom *told* me to be careful. Jiggling up and down, I waited, but the water didn't get very cold.

Ice! Ice would help.

I raced to the fridge and flung open the door.

A head was staring at me.

12

I screamed like a maniac.

A second later Charlie came rushing in. He saw the head and screamed even louder than me.

We took off down the hall and crashed through the front door. I don't remember my feet even touching the ground. Somehow we reached the car, and Charlie jumped behind the wheel. I dove into the backseat — right through Daniel. It was like passing through ice.

"What's wrong?" he asked.

"Here she comes!" cried Charlie, starting the engine.

Mrs. Rothbottom was moving fast.

I yelled, *"Drive! Drive!"*

Charlie pounded the gas pedal and took off.

"Did she remove the curse?" Daniel's voice sounded hard.

I looked out the back window. Mrs. Rothbottom was standing on the road watching us.

"What's a head doing in her fridge?" Charlie shrieked.

Daniel turned to me. "A head?"

"A gray one! It was *horrible*! She's a witch!"

I was shaking. "What was she going to do to Charlie? Cut his head off, too?"

"I don't know what a head is doing in her fridge, but Mrs. Rothbottom is someone you can trust."

"Maybe when *you* were alive. But things change. People change."

"You *must* go back or the curse won't be removed!"

"No *way* we're going back," I said. "We've got to tell the police."

"It's too late. Everything's closed."

"Police stations never close!"

"In this village they do. You'll have to wait until morning."

I slid down on the seat. My heart wouldn't stop thumping.

"And besides ..."

I sat up. "Besides *what*?"

"We have to get Charlie into water. It's almost midnight."

I looked at my watch. Eleven-thirty!

"We've got lots of time, Charlie." I tried to keep my voice calm. "Don't worry. We'll make it."

Charlie stared straight ahead.

"Charlie?"

He didn't answer.

"Let him be," said Daniel.

"What's wrong with him?"

"The mind shuts down at times ... to protect itself from going crazy."

I whispered, "But how can he drive?"

"He's on automatic pilot. People do it all the time."

Charlie didn't blink. Not even once. Just kept his eyes on the road and drove through the village. It wasn't until I felt the car going up the hill at the edge of town that it hit me where we were going. "We can't go back to the manor!"

Daniel frowned. "Why not?"

"Cornelius! That's why not!"

"Cornelius is harmless."

"He's done something to our mom! He *lied* about where she was."

"Listen to me, Lacey. Cornelius loves people and he wants to take care of them. He won't harm your mother, or you, or Charlie. That's a promise."

"Then why —"

Daniel cut me off. "We have to get Charlie into water and there's nowhere else to go."

———

When we got back to the manor, Cornelius saw Charlie and knew right away that something was wrong.

"What's happened to him?"

"I think he's just scared," I said. "I'm not sure."

Cornelius looked at Charlie with the most loving eyes I've ever seen. "I'm here, Charlie, and I'm going to take care of you." He put his arm around my brother's shoulders and gently led him toward the manor. "Everything will be fine. There's nothing to worry about. Nothing at all."

Nothing to worry about? Where was Mom? Was Mrs. Rothbottom a witch? Why did Daniel care so much about getting the curse removed?

Okay, the questions would have to wait. We had to get Charlie into water before midnight.

13

Cornelius helped Charlie up the winding staircase. When we got to the second floor, he led us straight to the locked room.

"What's in there?" I asked.

"This is Mr. Darcy's bedroom. Charlie will be comfortable sleeping here." He slid a key out of his pocket. "Everything's set up."

Set up? I wondered what he meant.

Cornelius pushed open the door and flicked on the light. There was a dresser in the corner, a fireplace with a gold clock on the mantel and tons of pictures all over the walls. Every picture was of a lady with long black hair: Catherine Manridge.

The room looked like a regular bedroom, except for one thing: beside the four-poster bed was a coffin — or at least it looked like a coffin — filled with clear water.

"Is ... is that where Uncle Jonathan slept?"

Cornelius nodded. "Every night of his life for

the past seventy years." He slid Charlie's jacket off. "A thermostat keeps it at body temperature ... nice and cozy."

The coffin had a white lining, a thick brown frame made of leather and on each side was a golden angel.

As Cornelius undressed Charlie, we both noticed that Charlie's jeans were wet. He must've been so scared he peed himself. I felt embarrassed for him, but Cornelius just slipped them off, rolled them up and told me to get a bottle from the top drawer of the dresser. "Pour a little into the water and swish it around," he said.

"What is it?"

"A special lotion that helps the body maintain its natural oils."

I pulled the cork out and poured a little into the water. When I swished it around, the whole room smelled like flowers. My eyes closed and I breathed deeply. Wonderful.

Then the clock started chiming.

It was midnight.

"You must get in the water now, Charlie," said Cornelius in a gentle voice. He slipped off Charlie's glasses and walked him the few steps to the coffin.

Charlie stepped in and lay down. The water

completely covered his chest, but his head was lifted a little, on some kind of pillow, I guessed.

Cornelius gathered up Charlie's clothes and left. I sat on the edge of the bed and stared down at my brother. I couldn't believe how calm he was. Daniel must've been right when he said the mind shuts down.

But then I noticed them — tears.

The lump in my throat hurt so bad I wanted to rip it out. Charlie hadn't done anything to deserve this. All he ever wanted was a little money so life could be a bit easier for us. Mom worked really hard, but there was never enough.

I whispered, "It's gonna be okay. I don't know how, but I know it's gonna be okay."

Charlie just stared at the ceiling. I could tell he'd given up.

<hr />

I turned out the light and crawled into bed with my clothes on. No way could I sleep. Over and over my mind kept asking, *Why is this happening? Why did I give Charlie the bottle?*

From where I was lying I could see a bookshelf. My eyes scanned the titles: *The Power of Faith, Have Courage, You Never Walk Alone.* Uncle

Jonathan must've had a lot of time to read all those years he was cursed. My mind could hardly wrap around it — practically a whole lifetime of having to sleep in water, of never being able to go out at night, of being alone. What a *horrible* way to live. I promised myself I'd never complain again.

At three in the morning I was still awake listening to the clock tick. Reading always puts me to sleep, so I flicked on the lamp at the far side of the bed, got up and pulled a book off the shelf. It had a dark purple cover with gold letters, *Words of Wisdom*. I snuggled back under the covers and started flipping through the pages. They were full of things people said when bad things happened to them. I spotted a picture of Mahatma Gandhi. Under the picture it said, "Whenever you are confronted with an opponent, conquer him with love."

Yeah. Right.

I turned the page. A bookmark slid out. It had a 3-D picture of a lantern on it. If you held the bookmark one way the lantern was off, but if you moved it just a little the light inside came on. It read, "One lamp serves to dispel a thousand years of darkness."

As I read on, my eyes got heavier and heavier.

Perfect ... I was finally ... falling ... asleep. So glad.

A loud knock jolted me awake.

"Did you hear that, Charlie?"

Charlie's eyes were closed.

There was another knock, even louder. Charlie still didn't wake up.

I pushed the blankets away. "Cornelius?"

Someone was whispering.

"Cornelius? Is that you?"

I slid off the bed and walked slowly over to the door. I was too scared to open it, so I leaned my ear against the keyhole and listened.

"H-e'-s n-o-t t-e-l-l-i-n-g t-h-e t-r-u-t-h. H-e-'s n-o-t t-e-l-l-i-n-g t-h-e t-r-u-t-h."

Panic washed over me. Without thinking I swung open the door. The boy I'd seen on the rocking chair hovered right in front of me!

He looked as scared as I was, and after a second he streaked down the stairs. I took off after him.

When I got to bottom I screeched to a stop. What was I thinking? *Go back to the room!* my mind shrieked.

Just as I was about to head back up, I heard something. My body froze. Humming. Someone was humming. *Mom?*

My heart pounded like crazy as my feet moved toward the sound. I could see golden light flickering at the far end of the corridor. Please, please, let it be Mom.

As I neared the last door the humming got louder. It was a man's voice. My heart sank.

I slowly poked my head around the frame and saw Cornelius standing next to a fireplace big enough to walk into. He was ironing. It took me a minute before I recognized the clothes. They were Charlie's. Cornelius was ironing Charlie's clothes in the middle of the night — and he looked happy.

I quietly made my way back upstairs, looking over my shoulder the whole time just in case the ghost that had streaked down decided to streak back up. Inside Uncle Jonathan's room I locked the door, dragged a chair over and jammed it under the doorknob. Then I jumped back into bed, pulling the covers up to my chin.

A couple of seconds later I pulled them down again.

Who wasn't telling the truth?

14

When the clock finally chimed seven I looked over the side of the bed.

"You okay, Charlie?"

"I'm okay, Lacey. Do you think it's all right if I get up now?"

"I'm not sure. Maybe stay until —"

A knock at the door made me gasp. *"Who's there?"*

"Cornelius Twickenham. May I come in?"

I relaxed, pulled the chair away from the door and unlocked it.

Cornelius stepped in, Charlie's clothes folded neatly on one hand and a big white towel on the other.

"Good morning," he said cheerily.

"Is it okay if I get up?" Charlie asked.

"Of course. At the rising of the sun, everything goes back to normal."

Charlie lifted his right hand and looked at it. Nothing happened so he pushed himself out of the water. Cornelius wrapped the towel around him and rubbed his arms, the way Mom used to when we were little.

"Just come down to the kitchen when you're ready," said Cornelius. "I've made pancakes, maple bacon, buttered toast with orange marmalade, country potatoes and a pot of hot chocolate ... *with* marshmallows."

Charlie grinned at him. It felt good to see him smile.

The second the door closed, Daniel appeared, sitting on the bed.

"Sleep well?"

"Yeah, right," grumbled Charlie, reaching for his glasses.

"Don't worry. I *know* we can get the curse removed. You'll be at home sleeping in your own bed soon. I promise."

Charlie sat on a chair and pulled on his socks. "I wish we were back there now."

That reminded me. "Where's our mom? She must be worried sick about us."

Daniel's body drifted across the bed and then he was standing.

"Your mother is safe. Please don't concern yourself."

"Where is she?"

"Sleeping soundly. I've put her in a trance so she won't go mad with worry about the curse."

Charlie bent to tie his sneakers. "He's right, Lacey. Mom's a big worrier."

"Then just tell us *where* she is."

"If I told you, you'd look for her, and there's still much to do," Daniel replied.

I yanked Charlie off the chair and made him stand beside me. "We're not moving until you tell us where she is."

"Let's get rid of the curse first. Then I'll show you. Promise." Daniel grinned.

I crossed my arms and gave him the dirtiest look I could.

His grin faded. "Very well. If you insist."

"I insist."

"Me, too," piped in Charlie.

Daniel moved over to the pool of water. He thought for a couple of seconds, then said, "This surface will do nicely."

Charlie and I moved closer. Daniel held his right hand over the water, and as he moved it in a circle, the water started swirling. When the swirling stopped we could see a picture, like on a TV. Mom was hovering in the air inside a dark room.

"There she is!" I shouted.

Charlie screamed, "She's dead!"

"Don't be ridiculous," snapped Daniel.

"She's dead! You killed her!" Charlie started bawling.

Daniel looked annoyed. "She's in suspended animation."

"I know dead when I see it!" wailed Charlie.

Just then Mom snored. Charlie grinned. "She lives!"

I breathed a sigh of relief.

"Now that we've determined your mother is alive and well," said Daniel, "may we focus on getting rid of the curse?"

Charlie and I nodded.

"Good." He smiled. "Now, the first thing we must do is ... eat!"

The smell of bacon drifted up the stairs.

Charlie sniffed. "Does Cornelius always cook such a great breakfast?"

"Always," said Daniel. "Ask for anything your heart desires and he'll make it. His one goal in life is to please."

When we got to the kitchen, the table was set and Cornelius stood holding a plate stacked high with pancakes. "Just say how many."

"Three for me," said Charlie, pulling out a chair.

"Three pancakes for Charlie Darcy." Cornelius slid them onto Charlie's plate.

"Hmm. Two for me, please," I said.

Cornelius slid two pancakes onto my plate, then turned to Daniel.

Daniel thought for a second. "Two slices of toasted, lightly buttered raisin bread, and eight strips of bacon. Extra crispy, if you please, Cornelius."

"Right away."

Daniel always talked like a grown-up.

As Cornelius dropped the raisin bread into the toaster he asked, "Will young Matthew be joining us this morning?"

"Who's Matthew?" Charlie asked.

"The other ghost," said Daniel, looking like he was smelling something bad. Then he looked at Cornelius. "Haven't seen him since yesterday. Hopefully he won't show up. He's been in a foul mood lately."

Cornelius placed a butter dish on the table. "I'll buy him something when I go to the village. That always makes him feel better."

Cooking for ghosts? Buying presents for ghosts? This really was a weird house.

I dug into my pancakes. They were amazing.

"Whenever the bacon's ready, so am I," said Charlie.

Cornelius's smile lit up the room.

Daniel pushed his plate to the side and rested his elbows on the table. "Now, about the curse."

In a flash, Cornelius's eyes turned dark.

"I think we should give Mrs. Rothbottom a second try," continued Daniel.

"Not a chance," I snapped.

"I'm with Lacey," mumbled Charlie through a mouthful of bacon. "Anybody with a head in their fridge is evil. No doubt about it. Evil. Evil. Evil."

Cornelius sat down beside us. "It's impossible to remove the curse. Mr. Darcy tried many times."

Daniel glared at him. "He told me he *didn't* try that hard because he felt he deserved it for betraying his best friend."

Cornelius turned away from him. "There's no need to torture yourselves trying to remove something that can't *be* removed. Just stay here. I'll take care of you." He looked at Charlie. "I assure you, sleeping in water isn't bad. It's comfortable, even soothing. You'll sleep like a baby. And during the day, why, you'll have *loads* of fun." His eyes swept over us. "You can play as much as you want, eat anything you want, *do* anything you want. You'll never have to go to school; you'll never have to work. I can give you a *wonderful* life."

A cupboard door suddenly slammed shut. Our heads jerked up. One by one, the other doors started opening and slamming really fast.

Charlie leaped out of his chair. "What's happening!"

"It's only Matty," said Daniel.

Drawers sprang open and forks and spoons crashed to the floor.

Daniel folded his arms in a sulk. "He just wants attention."

"*Go* to your chair, Matthew," said Cornelius in an angry voice.

Just like that, everything went dead quiet. Then a loud knock made us both jump.

Charlie spun around. "Who's that?"

Daniel smiled. "Mrs. Rothbottom."

"*What's she doing here?*"

"I rang her."

Cornelius looked furious. "Why are you meddling in things that are no longer your business?"

Another knock.

"Don't be rude, Cornelius," said Daniel. "Let the good lady in."

As he walked out of the kitchen, Cornelius's eyes shot daggers at Daniel.

Charlie panicked. "I gotta find someplace to hide!"

"Just listen to what Mrs. Rothbottom has to say," said Daniel. "That's all I ask."

"No!" Charlie dove under the table and pulled the chair in toward him. "She's a witch!"

15

Daniel disappeared just as Mrs. Rothbottom stepped in. She was carrying a big, round box that she plunked down on the table.

"Open it, Lacey."

"What's inside?"

"Just do as I say."

I slowly reached out and lifted the lid.

It was the head!

I screamed. Then Charlie screamed.

"Come out from under that table," said Mrs. Rothbottom.

"No."

"Don't be ridiculous, Charlie."

"Go away!"

"I'm here to explain this silly head. That's what caused the big kerfuffle, is it not?"

"What kerfuffle? There's no kerfuffle. We're just having breakfast — pancakes, bacon. Help yourself. Then go home."

"I've come to explain and I am not leaving until I do. Now, come out from under there this instant."

"I can hear fine from here," said Charlie. "No problem. No problem at all."

Mrs. Rothbottom's lips tightened. "Just feel it, Lacey. This head isn't real. What sort of person would keep a human head in her refrigerator?"

"You tell us."

Mrs. Rothbottom's right eyebrow went up. "It's made of *gelatin*."

"Gelatin? You mean, like, Jell-O?"

"Precisely. Taste it if you don't believe me."

"Don't taste it, Lacey!"

"I don't like Jell-O," I said. "Not when it looks like *that*."

"Oh, piddly-posh." Mrs. Rothbottom reached across the table and grabbed a spoon. She stuck it right in the head, lifted out a jiggly eyeball and ate it. "Delicious."

The chair moved and Charlie popped up.

"*Why?* Why would you make a Jell-O head?"

"It's my hobby. I create molds — unusual molds. I think I've outdone myself this time."

"Who is it?"

"Why, *Mr.* Rothbottom, of course."

Cornelius stepped into the doorway. "Please take your head and leave, madam. We have no need of your services."

"Then why did you call?"

"I beg your pardon?"

"You are Cornelius Twickenham, are you not?"

"I am. But I did not, and would not, call *you*."

"It's of no importance who called." Mrs. Rothbottom turned to Charlie. "If you care to come along, we can finish what we started last evening."

Charlie looked hopeful. "You mean, you can still remove the curse?"

"That is precisely what I mean."

"Great."

"It can't be done!" shouted Cornelius.

"Who are you to say what can or cannot be done, Mr. Twickenham?"

"You're a fake. You *all* are."

Mrs. Rothbottom's eyes narrowed. "We shall see."

Cornelius moved closer to Charlie. "She's building up your hopes, lad. But it will lead to nothing but disappointment. Terrible disappointment."

"It's okay, Cornelius," said Charlie. "I'll give it a shot. What've I got to lose?"

"Please don't go."

Cornelius sounded desperate.

"Go," whispered Daniel in my ear.

"Come on, Charlie."

Mrs. Rothbottom picked up her Jell-O head and we left. Our coats were still at her cottage, but at least Charlie could wear his scarf.

When I passed by the coat rack, it wasn't there.

16

In less than ten minutes we were walking through Mrs. Rothbottom's backyard. I heard Charlie ask, "How's it gonna work in the daytime? Without a full moon?"

"It will still work, I assure you."

She led us over to the tall tree. Then, just like last night, she told Charlie to face it. She lit both candles and told us to wait. This time *she* went into the house and came back holding the teapot with a towel. Resting it on a low wooden table, she gently lifted the lid. Steam swirled in the cold air.

"Now, let's get to it." She turned to me. "Lacey, I want you to hold Charlie's head. It must not touch the ground at *any* time. And you, Charlie, I want you to lie down on your back and look at the sky. Lacey will hold your head above the ground. It *mustn't* touch. Do you understand?"

Charlie nodded, got down in the snow and leaned back. I cradled his head, resting it on my knees.

"Thanks, Lacey" he said.

"His head cannot touch your knees," said Mrs. Rothbottom. "There must be space between it and the earth."

I shifted my legs back. Charlie's head got a lot heavier.

Mrs. Rothbottom untied a green velvet sack and pulled out a little bottle. I watched as she poured oil into her hands and rubbed them together, mumbling something I couldn't make out. She put the bottle back in the sack and took out a small hourglass with glistening white sand in it.

My arms started to ache. How could a head weigh so much?

Mrs. Rothbottom knelt on the ground beside us. "Charlie, I'm going to pour the tea potion in a circle around your body. But first I'll pour this blessed sand over your forehead. As I do, I'll recite a curse-breaking incantation. All you have to do is lie very, very still." She looked at me. "Remember, Lacey. Do *not* let his head touch the ground."

"I won't."

Mrs. Rothbottom unscrewed the cap at one end of the hourglass and dropped it beside her. It disappeared into the snow. She held the glass up. *"By the power of light, which is, and always will be, greater than the power of darkness, we ask that the curse placed upon Charlie Darcy be removed."*

She poured a circle of sand in the middle of Charlie's forehead.

"I now cleanse this child with the sands of time."

She poured more sand in the middle of the circle.

"With light and love and magic verse,
I turn around this wicked curse.
As these words of mine are spoken,
May this evil curse be broken."

She poured the last of the sand in a straight line going from the center of the circle up to the top of Charlie's head.

"This curse can now no longer be.
From its grasp ... you are set free."

A wave of peace washed over me. Charlie must've felt it too because he looked up and smiled. My eyes filled with tears. Happy tears.

"Charlie Darcy," continued Mrs. Rothbottom. "You are under universal light and protection. *Nothing* can harm you. The force behind this curse —"

A car horn honked.

My hands jerked.

Charlie's head hit the ground.

"Nooo!" shouted Mrs. Rothbottom.

Charlie rolled over. "My head touched the ground! It touched the ground!"

"I'm sorry! I'm sorry! The horn —"

Mrs. Rothbottom ran around the side of the cottage.

"Where's she going?" cried Charlie.

"I don't know."

"What am I gonna do *now*?"

I felt sick. How could I have let Charlie's head hit the ground?

We heard snow crunching. Mrs. Rothbottom came back into the yard looking furious. "We must act quickly."

She grabbed the teapot. "Come inside. *Immediately.*"

I helped Charlie up and we raced back into the kitchen. Mrs. Rothbottom put the pot on the table, flung open a cupboard over the sink and pushed dishes aside. Then she grabbed a tin cup and poured the tea into it so fast it splashed all over. She handed Charlie the cup. "Drink it!"

"*Drink* it? It's supposed to go on the ground!"

"Do as I say!"

"I'm afraid to drink it!"

"Do you wish to have the curse removed or not?" She spat out the words.

Charlie's hands shook as he put the cup to his lips. "It smells horrible!"

Mrs. Rothbottom wagged her finger at him. "Stop being a baby and drink. It will work, I assure you. Though you may lose your sight for a few days."

"I'm gonna be *blind*?"

"Are you sure there isn't another way?" I pleaded.

"It's the only way. So tell your brother to drink."

"Charlie. Just *drink* the darn thing!"

"I can't, Lacey! I can't!"

"Drink it!"

"It loses its potency in three minutes." Mrs. Rothbottom sat down. "And there are not enough ingredients to make another one."

Charlie glared at me, plugged his nose and drank. Coughing like crazy, he finally got his voice back. "Is ... is the curse gone?"

Mrs. Rothbottom quickly moved over to the window and pulled back the curtains. Her whole body relaxed. "The candles are out." She slowly turned to Charlie and smiled. "You're fine."

Charlie coughed some more. Mrs. Rothbottom walked over to him and rubbed his back. "I'm sorry, luv. It had to be done."

"Why'd Charlie have to *drink* the tea? You said —"

"His head touched the ground, Lacey. I warned you *not* to let that happen."

"I didn't do it on purpose. The horn scared me!"

"It scared us all. But his head *wasn't* to touch the ground."

"It *did* touch the ground! So how can you say the curse is gone?"

"I compensated."

"What does *that* mean?"

"With the protective tea *inside* Charlie instead of just around him, the curse has definitely been lifted."

She sounded so sure. I hoped with all my heart that she was right.

"Now, please pay me. There must be balance or it may not continue to work. Never take without giving."

Charlie and I emptied our pockets. Altogether we had $27. I remembered that the sign had said *Curses removed £40*. We didn't have enough.

Mrs. Rothbottom tucked the money in her sweater pocket. "Splendid."

When she saw the surprised look on my face, she winked.

The clock on the wall chimed. It was only eight o'clock in the morning, but Charlie's eyes started to close.

Mrs. Rothbottom walked him into the living room. "Let's let him sleep. That tea is very powerful."

"I sure hope it works."

She looked at me over her shoulder. "You'll see for yourself ... at midnight."

17

"If only I hadn't pulled my hands away when that car honked." I couldn't stop thinking about how I'd let Charlie down.

"It wasn't your fault, Lacey."

I stared out the window. "Shouldn't we phone Cornelius to come and get us?"

"No."

Why did she sound so mad? "Just in case," I said, "shouldn't Charlie be near the water bed?"

Mrs. Rothbottom opened a drawer and lifted out two metal molds. "Someone honked that horn on purpose."

"What?"

"I only saw it from a distance. But I believe it was Mr. Darcy's car."

"Cornelius?"

"For some reason that man does not want the curse removed. I'd rather you and Charlie stay here, for now."

She held up the mold pans. "Which one shall

I make? Her Royal Highness or King Kong?"

Before I could answer, the phone rang. Mrs. Rothbottom talked to somebody and then said, "Come right over. I have time today."

After she hung up, she smiled. "Now *there* is a spell I can cast."

"For what?"

"Love. It's one of the easiest. Everyone wants to love and be loved. People need a little nudge, that's all."

Mrs. Rothbottom made us some hot chocolate, then got to work mixing the Jell-O and pouring it in the King Kong mold. As she slid it into the fridge, we heard a knock.

"That will be Miss Briar."

She went to the door and came back with a white-haired lady wearing a bright red dress. I thought Miss Briar would be a whole lot younger, but I guess old people want love, too.

In a thick Scottish accent Miss Briar said, "Hello. How are you today?"

I wanted to say, Terrible! My brother's cursed! My mom's missing! And we're living with ghosts! What I said was, "Fine. Thank you."

Miss Briar turned to Mrs. Rothbottom. "You're very kind to take me on such short notice. Very kind, indeed."

"No problem at all." Mrs. Rothbottom smiled and opened the door that led downstairs. "Come along."

When they'd gone, I wandered into the living room and slumped down in an armchair. I wished Charlie'd wake up and talk to me, but he was snoring peacefully. It was probably better this way. When you're awake, you worry.

"I'm all right most days, but sometimes the sadness comes over me."

It was Miss Briar's voice. How could I hear her from the basement?

I followed the sound to a metal grate on the floor.

"Do you really think there's a chance I'll find love again? I'm so old."

"Nonsense," said Mrs. Rothbottom. "You have many good years ahead of you."

I knelt down and pressed my ear against the grate.

"I ... I don't want to *force* anyone to love me."

"Don't you worry about that," said Mrs. Rothbottom. "Love spells can't *make* someone love you. At least, not the ones I cast." Then she said, "On this piece of paper, write 'Bring me my true love' seven times."

About a minute later she said, "Now, Miss Briar, turn the paper upside down and write your name on it ... then sprinkle it with this powder and run your nails down the middle."

As I listened, my eyes got heavier and heavier.

———

"Wake up, sleepyhead."

Mrs. Rothbottom was leaning over me. I was still on the floor, but there was a pillow under my head.

"Where's Miss Briar?"

"She left hours ago."

"*Hours ago?* What time is it?"

"Almost midnight."

"You're kidding!" I scrambled up.

"Stay calm." She smiled at me. "We've got plenty of time."

"Where's your bathtub?"

The steps creaked as we climbed up to the second floor.

"It's the last room on the right," said Mrs. Rothbottom as we headed down the hall to the bathroom. It had a sink, a toilet and a small low tub, but the room was so small they barely fit.

"Where's Charlie?"

"Charlie who?"

My heart skipped a beat. "What do you mean, 'Charlie who?'"

Mrs. Rothbottom turned on the faucet. "Is that a friend of yours?"

"Why are you doing this!?"

She looked confused. "Doing what, luv?"

"Acting like you don't know what's going on!"

Her hand tested the water. "Tell me what's going on, Lacey."

"You're scaring me, Mrs. Rothbottom."

"Don't be scared. I'm just running your bath."

"*My* bath?"

She looked up at me. "You're cursed, remember?"

"Wake up!"

It was Charlie's voice.

"Wake up, Lacey! Wake up!"

"Where are you, Charlie?"

"Right here. I'm right here. Just open your eyes."

"My eyes are open!"

Cold water splashed on my face.

Mrs. Rothbottom was leaning over me again.

"Where's Charlie?" I shouted.

"I'm here."

Charlie stepped out from behind Mrs. Rothbottom. His face was all black and shrivelled.

18

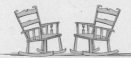

Someone shook me hard. "Wake up!"

My eyes popped open and I saw Charlie.

"Are you okay, Lacey? I couldn't get you to wake up."

"I must've fallen asleep. Had a bad dream." I rubbed my eyes and looked around. I was still on the living room floor. "I always have bad dreams when I sleep in the afternoon."

"It isn't afternoon anymore." Mrs. Rothbottom was standing in the doorway.

I looked at my watch. It was ten minutes to midnight. "We gotta get Charlie upstairs!"

"The curse is gone." Mrs. Rothbottom said in a gentle voice. "I assure you."

"Just in case, can we get him close to water? *Please?*"

Mrs. Rothbottom nodded. "Of course."

We headed up to the second floor. The stairs creaked, just like they did in my dream. Something else was weird. Mrs. Rothbottom pointed and said, "It's the last room on the right."

That was in my dream, too.

"Go ahead. I'll be right with you."

Charlie and I kept going.

"The tub's already filled," said Charlie. "She knew you were worried about me."

"Aren't *you* worried?"

"Nope. Don't ask me why, but I feel great."

I felt a bit better when I saw the bathroom. It didn't look like the one in my dream. This one had lots of room, a big window and a tub with feet like claws.

Mrs. Rothbottom brushed past us, holding a small clock. She set it on the windowsill, then put the toilet lid down and sat on it. "In six short minutes you'll see that everything is back to normal."

We waited.

Two minutes to go.

One minute.

Whatever was in that tea made Charlie cool as a cucumber. Maybe everything *was* all right now. Or maybe it wasn't.

"Take your clothes off, Charlie."

"Why?"

"Just in case. Please. Take them off."

Charlie rolled his eyes, but slipped them off. "There. You happy?"

The second hand on the clock moved to the last thirty seconds. Twenty-nine ... twenty-eight ... twenty-seven ...

Mrs. Rothbottom tore off some toilet paper and blew her nose.

Eight seconds ... seven ... six ... five ... four ...

My heart was in my throat.

Three ... two ... one.

Nothing happened.

The clock kept ticking.

"See?" said Charlie.

My whole body relaxed and I laughed. Then I grabbed my brother and hugged him hard. "You're okay! You're okay!"

"Ow!"

"Sorry. I'm just so happy!"

"Ow!" he cried again.

I wasn't even touching him.

"What's wrong?"

He stared at his hands. They were turning black. And cracking. The cracks spread really fast up his arms.

"Get in the water!" I shouted, pushing him in.

Charlie splashed down then tried to get up.

"Stay down!"

Charlie lay really still. I stared at his hands and arms under the water. The cracks filled up and the black color disappeared.

"I'm still cursed!" screamed Charlie. *"I'm still cursed!"*

19

I glared at Mrs. Rothbottom. "You said the curse was gone!"

Her face looked really pale. "It ... it should be."

"*Should be?*" I shrieked. "*Well, it's not!*"

"Something's wrong. Something's very wrong." She headed out the door.

"*Don't go!*" I pleaded.

"I have to think."

She stuck her head back in. "Hold his hand. Hold it tightly."

I quickly knelt down beside the tub, reached under the water and grabbed Charlie's hand. "It's gonna be okay, Charlie. I promise. It's gonna be okay."

Charlie's hand was trembling. He looked terrified.

A minute later Mrs. Rothbottom marched back in.

"I know you're frightened, Charlie, and you've every right to be. But I want you to think, and think hard." She sat down again. "Did anyone take your picture while you were at the manor?"

"No."

"Did you clip your nails?"

"No."

"Did you bang your hand against something and *break* a nail?"

"No."

"Did anyone cut your hair or clean your hairbrush?"

I couldn't stand it anymore. "Why are you asking such stupid questions?!"

Mrs. Rothbottom turned her head. "Because the only time a curse cannot be removed is when someone has put roots on the cursed person."

"Roots? What are you talking about?"

"A trick has been laid."

"Who'd play a trick on Charlie?"

"Not played. *Laid.* A trick has been laid. I'm sure of it."

"You're talking crazy!"

"I'm not. If someone wants to control you to keep you from doing something, or *make* you do something, they lay a trick on you. They take personal items — clothing or a picture, perhaps. Hair and nail clippings work best, though, because they're part of your body. Whatever it is, it's in a bag and hidden. If a trick *has* been laid, curse removals won't work. Part of you is somewhere else, so the curse remains. It's still attached. Do you understand?"

"Who would do that?" I asked.

Mrs. Rothbottom looked from me to Charlie. "My guess is Cornelius Twickenham."

Charlie sat up. *"Cornelius?"*

His chest and arms started to crack.

"Stay in the water!" Mrs. Rothbottom shouted.

Charlie quickly went back down. *"Why?* Why would he do that? He *likes* me."

"I don't know why. Not yet, anyway."

"Remember, Charlie? At breakfast this morning? Cornelius didn't want us to remove the curse."

Charlie nodded. "He said he'd look after us. Give us *anything* we wanted. He even said we wouldn't have to go to school."

Mrs. Rothbottom slowly leaned back. "This is starting to make sense. Mr. Twickenham was Mr. Darcy's caretaker for so many years. Now, with him gone, he has no one to look after." She turned her head toward us. "He's lonely. The poor man is lonely."

I suddenly remembered. "Charlie's *scarf.*"

Mrs. Rothbottom frowned. "What scarf, Lacey?"

"Charlie came here without his scarf! But he didn't *forget* it. It wasn't on the hook where Cornelius put it when we first got there!"

"Aha! That could well be it. And scarves *always* have a hair or two on them."

"Then it *was* Cornelius. *He* laid the trick on Charlie."

"Good. Now that we know, we can do something about it."

"What?" asked Charlie. "What can we do?"

"Why, find the trick, of course. And destroy it."

"And just how are we gonna do that?"

"The two of you must go back to Blaxston Manor."

Charlie shook his head, splashing water around. "I'm not going back. No way. You can't make me."

"You mustn't be afraid. No one will harm you, I promise."

"Oh, yeah? Like you promised the curse was removed? What if Cornelius does something *else* to me? Forget it. I'm staying here, thank you very much."

"Cornelius wants the curse to remain," said Mrs. Rothbottom. "If it's broken, he'll have no one to look after. Loneliness can make a person do terrible things."

I remembered how it felt when our dad died. Charlie and I felt lonely for a long time. So did Mom.

I straightened my shoulders. "What does a trick look like?"

Mrs. Rothbottom smiled. "That's the spirit, Lacey."

She got up and left the bathroom.

Charlie lifted his head a bit. "*Now* where's she going?"

When Mrs. Rothbottom came back she was holding three bags — a red one, a white one and a black one.

"These are mojo bags," she said. "They're made of flannel and, as you can see, they come in different colors. Mojo bags are most often used to lay *good* tricks — for money, blessings or love. But they can also be used to *prevent* something from happening. Mr. Twickenham obviously collected items from you, Charlie, and put them into a bag like this. Then he hid it. Your job is to find it."

"Find it where?" cried Charlie. "That house is *huge*."

"It won't be just lying about, that's for certain. You must look everywhere you can think of — under things, behind things, *inside* things. Some people hide tricks indoors; others bury them outside. So look *everywhere*."

"If we find it, then what do we do?" I asked.

"Listen carefully. When you find the trick, *immediately* fill a bathtub with hot water. Then mix nine teaspoons of salt into the water." She turned to Charlie. "Take off all your clothes and step in and out of the bath nine times. *Exactly* nine times. Each time you step into the tub, wash yourself with the salty water, rubbing *away* from your head and moving downward. Never rub upward. *Never.* Do you understand?"

Charlie nodded. "Yeah."

"When you step out after the ninth wash, fill a bowl with the salted bath water, go outside and throw it toward the sun — or the moon, depending on what time it is."

"That gets rid of the trick?" I asked.

"Yes, indeed. However, *after* that ritual is completed, the bag and all its contents must be destroyed. Either burn it or throw it into running water ... perhaps a river or stream."

Charlie looked up at me. "There's a river under the bridge! Remember, Lacey?"

"Excellent," said Mrs. Rothbottom. "When you've gotten rid of the trick, ring me. I'll pick you up and we can remove the curse."

"Do I have to drink that horrible tea again?"

"Not this time," Mrs. Rothbottom replied. "We shall pour it around you this time, Charlie — *if* we can trust Lacey to hold your head more carefully."

"I won't screw up again. I promise."

20

Mrs. Rothbottom brought me a blanket and pillow, then went to bed. I stayed with Charlie for the rest of the night, but neither of us could sleep. He kept asking, "Why me? Why'd this have to happen to *me*?"

"Mrs. Rothbottom knows what she's doing." I squeezed his hand. "Everything's going to be all right. This'll be over soon, and we'll be back in our own beds. I know it. I just know it."

Charlie looked so tired. If only he could sleep. But how do you sleep when you're terrified?

The minutes ticked by so slowly. I lay down on the floor and pulled the blanket around me. "Dad, if you can hear me, *please* help us."

Somehow the night passed. When morning light poured in the window, I helped Charlie out of the tub. As he dried himself off and got dressed, I noticed his fingers were white and crinkly, but I didn't say anything.

We headed downstairs.

A note was on the table, leaning against the pepper shaker: *"Call Cornelius — his number's by the phone. Tell him the curse was not removed and you wish to go home."*

"Where'd she go?" Charlie sounded really mad.

"Maybe something important came up." I ripped her number from the bottom of the note and stuck it in my pocket. "Let's just do what she says."

In the living room Charlie picked up the phone, took a deep breath and dialed.

I whispered, "Pretend you're really upset that the curse wasn't removed."

"Pretend?"

As soon as Cornelius came on the line, Charlie burst out crying. "It didn't work, Cornelius! I'm still cursed!" I leaned in and listened. "I was *sure* it'd work. Mrs. Rothbottom said —"

"They all *say* they can help. But I've never seen it work. Not once."

"What should I do?" Charlie sobbed.

"Come home, lad. Come home."

"Will you pick me and Lacey up?"

"It will be my pleasure."

Charlie slipped off his glasses and wiped his eyes with the back of his hand. I guess he wasn't acting after all.

We put our coats on and waited in front of the cottage. When Cornelius came he stepped out of the car and opened the back door for us, like we were really special. I thought he'd ask us all kinds of questions, but he didn't say a word.

We drove silently through the village. People were out walking, opening up their shops. Everything looked normal. Would anything be normal for me and Charlie again?

As we bounced over the bridge I suddenly panicked. What if the river was frozen?

It wasn't. Good.

Cornelius turned in to the driveway. Through the front windshield I could see the rocking chairs. They were moving back and forth. We circled around the manor and stopped near the tree with the swing. Cornelius got out quickly and opened the door for us again. He was acting like he was our servant, and I didn't like it. Charlie didn't even notice — he just kept his head down and walked to the house.

When we stepped inside, something smelled awesome. Charlie's head went up. "What's that?"

"Freshly baked peanut butter cookies with toasted walnuts and dollops of sweet Belgian chocolate." Cornelius had such a huge grin on his face that his eyes crinkled up. "I set them out to cool before I left. Come along."

With a quick step he led us to the kitchen. We didn't even stop to take our coats off — just grabbed cookies.

"This is the *best* cookie I've ever tasted." I wasn't lying. It *was*.

Charlie made some *mmmm* sounds and nodded.

"I never had children of my own," said Cornelius, walking over to the fridge. "So it gives me great pleasure to do things for you."

He poured two glasses of milk. I remembered what Mrs. Rothbottom said about Cornelius being lonely, and felt sorry for him. "Do you have any brothers or sisters?"

Cornelius slowly lowered the milk bottle. "I'm quite alone." He stared at the glasses for a really long time, then finally put them in front of us. "I believe I hear Matthew calling. Please excuse me."

I could tell my question had upset him, but I didn't know what to say.

As he walked out of the kitchen, Daniel appeared.

"It didn't work!" shouted Charlie. "I'm still cursed!"

"I assumed so, since you're back."

"Somebody's put a —"

I waved my hands. "Shh!"

Charlie stopped.

I went over, stuck my head into the dining room and looked around. "Okay. Coast is clear."

"Somebody laid a *trick* on me," continued Charlie. "And Mrs. Rothbottom thinks it's Cornelius!"

"A trick." Daniel leaned back. "I never thought of that."

Charlie reached for another cookie. "You know what a trick is?"

"Nail clippings, strands of hair, personal items. And Cornelius would be just the one to do it. He makes no bones about not wanting the curse removed."

"We've got to find where Cornelius hid it," I said. "Then we have to throw it in the river."

"I'll help you look."

"I figured maybe you'd know where it was," said Charlie, "being a ghost and all."

"If I didn't see where he put it, I have no way of knowing. But I'm sure he'd hide it well."

"Any ideas?" I asked.

"His room would be my first guess. I'll go and check."

"Look for a mojo bag with a brown scarf in it."

"Will do."

Daniel disappeared.

While we waited for him to check out Cornelius's room, Charlie and I opened every drawer and cupboard in the kitchen. I even looked inside the fridge.

That gave me an idea. I opened it again and took out the carton of eggs.

"What're you doing, Lacey?"

"We can search better if Cornelius isn't in the house."

"Yeah, but what're you *doing*?"

Footsteps.

"He's coming!"

I panicked, yanked open the cupboard above the fridge and threw the carton inside. The eggs cracked really loud just as Cornelius came in. I coughed to cover the sound.

"That's a nasty cough you have there, Lacey," he said.

"I think I caught a cold at Mrs. Rothbottom's." I coughed a bit more. "We were outside in the snow without our coats."

Cornelius shook his head. "That woman is a menace."

Charlie was staring at something. I casually looked over — slimy yellow goo was sliding out the bottom of the cupboard. Coughing like crazy, I staggered over to the table.

"Oh, my," said Cornelius. "We're going to have to do something about that."

He went to the fridge and pulled out a small black bottle. "This should do the trick."

"What is it?"

"Echinacea with goldenseal, wild indigo, myrrh, bee propolis and cayenne pepper."

"I ... I can't swallow pills. They make me gag."

"Not a problem." He unscrewed the little black top. "These are drops. You can either take them directly under your tongue or mixed with water."

Egg goo hung an inch from his head.

"Under my tongue!" I shouted so loud it made him jump.

"All right, then." He stepped toward me just as the goo landed on the back of his jacket. I was so relieved that I opened my mouth and let him put the drops in.

They had to be poison. My eyes bugged out and I gasped and hacked and thought I was going to die.

"I know. I know. It tastes terrible." Cornelius screwed the cap back on. "But it works. You'll see."

Charlie smirked. "Now you know how I felt."

Long strings of yellow goo were hanging from the cupboard. Any second Cornelius would see them. Charlie and I had to do something, fast. I motioned with my head toward the window.

"Cornelius! Come here! Come here!" Charlie shouted, running over to the window.

Cornelius followed him.

Charlie pointed out the window into the yard. "Look at that!"

While they had their backs turned, I grabbed a dish towel and started madly wiping up the goo.

"What exactly are we looking at?" asked Cornelius.

"Don't you see it? A fox. A big, fat fox. See? Right there by the swing!"

"A fox?" Cornelius sounded surprised. "There aren't any foxes in this area."

"Well, maybe it isn't a fox. Maybe it's a … skunk."

Cornelius laughed. "It was probably a badger, Charlie, although they don't normally come out during the day. We've had no end of trouble with them this winter. The miserable creatures dig tunnels everywhere."

He started to turn. I waved frantically. Charlie grabbed Cornelius and swung him back around.

"There it is again!"

"Where?"

"Up there! In the tree! He's doing a handstand!"

"A *handstand*? Where?"

"Right *there*! One, two, three, four, five — five branches up, on the left side!"

"I'm sorry. But I still don't see anything."

I cleared my throat as an "all clear" signal.

"That's one smart badger," said Charlie. "He keeps hiding."

"Well, just stay inside until he moves on," said Cornelius. "They can be fierce."

"Inside. No problem."

Daniel appeared at the door. "Anyone for mini-golf?"

Charlie and I raced out of the kitchen and pounded down the stairs like we were really excited about playing mini-golf. But the second we got to the arcade, Daniel led us to a room behind a curtain. It was a movie theater with a concession stand that had tons of chocolate bars, red licorice twists, jelly beans, suckers and a giant gum-ball machine.

"Did you find the trick?" I asked.

Daniel looked sad. "You're not going to believe this."

Charlie's eyes opened wide. "*What?* What won't we believe?"

"I did find a trick —"

Charlie danced around. "Yes! Yes! I'm free!"

"However ..."

Charlie stopped dancing.

"However *what*?"

"It wasn't the trick laid on you."

"What d'ya *mean* not the one laid on me!"

Daniel glared at him. "Lower your voice."

"What d'ya *mean* not the one laid on me?" Charlie whispered.

"Inside a locked box at the back of Cornelius's closet I found a black mojo bag containing nail clippings, wisps of hair, a pair of gloves ... and a photograph."

"A photograph of *who*?" I asked.

He glanced over his shoulder and then whispered, "Jonathan."

21

"*Uncle Jonathan?*" Charlie and I said together.

"Why?" shouted Charlie. "Why would Cornelius lay a trick on Uncle Jonathan?"

I whacked him. "Shhh!"

"It doesn't make any *sense*."

"Actually … it does," said Daniel. "If the curse was removed, your uncle would have been able to lead a normal life — marry, have children, go out anytime he wished. But the curse" — Daniel's eyes narrowed — "forced him to stay in this miserable manor, dependent on Cornelius for everything."

I couldn't believe it. "Cornelius made Uncle Jonathan suffer his whole life for nothing."

Daniel nodded. "This confirms what I've believed for some time now." He looked from me to Charlie. "Cornelius is mad."

"You mean *crazy?*"

I clamped my hand over Charlie's mouth.

He pulled away. "We gotta get outta here!

Right *now*. Let's run to the village. Somebody there will help us!"

"We must first find the trick." Daniel sounded hard. "Or Mrs. Rothbottom will not be able to remove your curse."

"Where'd she go, anyway? She left us at her house all alone. She's up to something. I can feel it in my bones, and my bones never lie."

"Charlie's right," I said. "It doesn't make sense that she'd just leave."

The lights went out.

I gasped.

A low rumbling sound came from the floor under our feet. "What's happening?" Charlie cried.

The sound got louder and louder. Then the room started shaking.

"Matty!" Daniel shouted. "Stop these theatrics!"

But it didn't stop. The whole room shook so hard Charlie and I had to hang onto the seats.

It felt as if an earthquake had hit — and it kept getting worse.

"T-h-e-y c-a-n h-e-l-p m-e!"

"Matty!" Daniel sounded very grown up. "Go to your chair this instant!"

Just like that, the shaking stopped.

Charlie's face was white as a sheet. "Is ... is he gone?"

"Yes, he's gone. Everything's all right now."

Charlie looked all around. "Why does everybody keep telling him to go to his chair?"

"The movement soothes him."

Suddenly, the curtains flew open and a rocking chair flew straight at us. Charlie and I yelled and jumped out of the way. The chair passed right through Daniel, crashing against the wall. Then Matty appeared, hovering right in front of us. He shrieked, "I w-a-n-t t-o g-o h-o-m-e!"

Charlie's eyes rolled up into his head, and he fainted.

"Not again! Charlie ... Charlie!" I crouched beside him. "Daniel —"

He'd disappeared.

Charlie started to come around.

"I'm here, Charlie. I'm here. Are you okay?"

"Who *was* that?"

I straightened his glasses and helped him up. "Matty."

Charlie was shaking. "As if we don't have enough problems." He reached for a Snickers bar. "What are we gonna do, Lacey?"

"First, we have to find the trick that was laid on you."

He took a huge bite. "When Cornelius sees us

poking around he's gonna get suspicious." He grabbed a Mars bar.

"I've got a plan."

"What plan?"

"You keep Cornelius busy while I look for the trick."

"Busy how?" he asked between bites.

"Play with him — play cards or charades or something."

"That's *it*? Play with a crazy person? That's your plan?"

"He isn't crazy."

"Daniel said he was!"

"Daniel doesn't know *everything*. You've heard about people being insanely jealous, but it doesn't mean they're really insane. Cornelius is just lonely, like Mrs. Rothbottom said. And that's made him do stupid things."

"Nice try. But I still don't want to play with him."

"Well, it's all I can think of. If you've got a better idea, just say so."

The curtain opened. Daniel hissed, "Mini-golf!"

Charlie and I raced through the arcade over to the mini-golf course. Daniel whipped some clubs at us and we started swinging.

"Bravo," he said, sitting on top of a windmill and clapping.

Cornelius came over. "I forgot to ask if you had breakfast at Mrs. Rothbottom's."

"No," said Charlie. "And I'm starving — starving to death — withering away to nothing."

"Just tell me what you'd like."

Charlie started to answer, but I cut him off. "French toast. Charlie and I would *love* French toast."

Cornelius nodded. "French toast it is. Breakfast will be ready in eleven and a half minutes."

"Great. Thanks, Cornelius. You're amazing."

After Cornelius left, Charlie looked at me. "What was *that* about?"

"There aren't any eggs, remember?"

"So how's he gonna make French toast without any eggs?"

"That's the point."

Charlie frowned. "*What's* the point?"

"He'll have to go and *buy* some," I said. "That'll get him out of the house while we look for the trick."

"Smart girl," said Daniel.

A couple of minutes later Cornelius came back. "I was certain I had some eggs but there's nary a one. Is there something else you'd like?"

"Aw, maaan," said Charlie. "I had my heart *set* on French toast."

I hung my head like I was really disappointed, too. "It's our favorite."

"French toast it will be, then," said Cornelius. "I can drive to the village. No problem at all."

"You'd do that for us?" Charlie smiled sweetly.

"It will be my pleasure."

"You're terrific, Cornelius. A real pal."

Cornelius went back upstairs. We waited a minute, then raced across the arcade, crept up the steps and listened. When we heard the car come around to the front we peeked out a window. Cornelius drove off.

"He's gone. Charlie, let's split up and start looking. We only have about fifteen minutes."

Daniel appeared. "We have longer than that. I put a nail in his tire. It'll be flat as one of his pancakes by the time he gets to the village."

"Way to go, Daniel." Charlie tried to give him a high-five, but Daniel looked confused.

"All right," I said. "Charlie, you look around this floor, and I'll search the second floor. Daniel, you check high shelves and inside things that are locked."

We all took off.

22

When I got to the second floor, I figured there wasn't any point in searching Uncle Jonathan's room — that'd be the last place Cornelius would hide anything.

I moved past it to the next one. It didn't take long to figure out that this was Cornelius's room. The closet was full of butler uniforms and the shiniest shoes I'd ever seen.

A head came through the wall. I gasped.

Daniel grinned. "Don't bother. I've already checked this room." His head disappeared.

As I turned to leave, my eye caught a black-and-white picture taped to the back of the door. Four boys were in it, all of them smiling. The oldest looked about fourteen or fifteen and had his arms wrapped around the smaller ones.

I called out, "Daniel?"

His head came through the closet ceiling. "That's Cornelius and his brothers."

"But he said —"

"He lied."

Daniel vanished again.

"Why'd he lie?" I yelled.

Daniel's whole body appeared this time.

"Cornelius rarely speaks of it, but after his parents died he was forced to take care of his brothers. One day there was a fire and all were lost — except him. He never forgave himself."

"Was it his fault?"

"He fell asleep with a candle burning. The curtains caught fire, and the whole place went up like a tinderbox."

"That's *awful*."

"It is. However, it explains his obsession with wishing to care for people."

"Mrs. Rothbottom said he's lonely, not crazy."

"She's quite right, of course. I overstated."

"It's still not right, though," I said. "I mean, what he did to Uncle Jonathan."

"Thank you, Lacey."

"For what?"

Daniel cleared his throat. "For being so kindhearted toward your uncle. You didn't even know him."

"I know the difference between right and wrong. And what Cornelius did was wrong."

"It's too late to help your uncle, but it's not too late to help your brother. Let's keep looking, shall we?"

He disappeared.

I searched the next room, checking under the bed, through drawers, even inside the fireplace. When I opened what I thought was the closet, I was surprised to see a sunroom filled with tons of plants. Every one of them was dead.

Huge spiderwebs stretched across the room and covered all the windows. If the *webs* were this big ...

I stepped back. Too late.

Spiders.

Crawling toward me! *Thousands of them!*

I slammed the door, but they came underneath it. Stomping like crazy, I killed as many as I could, but they kept coming and coming! Before I freaked out completely, I grabbed some pillows from the bed and shoved them up against the opening.

Slowly, I inched my hands away.

More spiders!

I pressed down hard on the pillows. That stopped them. Looking around, I spotted some logs stacked beside the fireplace. I dragged one over with my foot and rolled it onto the pillows. It worked, for now anyway.

I dashed out of the room and across the hall to another bedroom. It took a couple of minutes before my heart stopped thumping, but I continued looking around. This bedroom had a door beside the window with a sign that said **STAIRCASE 5**. I headed up. After about fifteen steps it ended at a brick wall.

The next room had a trapdoor in the floor. The brass plate near the bottom said **STAIRCASE 12**. It led down a flight of stairs and came out in a tiny room decorated like a doll's house.

I searched around. No mojo bag. Back up the stairs.

Just as I closed the trapdoor, I heard footsteps. Was Cornelius back already?

"Lacey? Where are you?" It was Charlie.

"In here."

Charlie came in holding a huge scroll. "Take a look at this." He unrolled it on the bed. "It's a family tree. Everybody's here — Grandma and Grandpa and their parents, all our aunts and uncles, and look ..." He pointed. "This is Mom, Dad and you." He tapped his finger on an empty square. "My picture's missing."

"Bet it's in the mojo bag." I said.

"That's what I think, too."

The window rattled. As we stared, the glass misted up.

Charlie grabbed my arm. "What's going on, Lacey?"

Before I could answer, two words appeared.

LOOK OUTSIDE

We ran downstairs and out the door into the backyard. It was like we were inside a cloud.

"Where'd this fog come from, Lacey?"

"I don't know."

"It wasn't here before."

"T-h-e-r-e's a b-o-g n-e-a-r-b-y."

We spun around. A boy appeared in the fog.

"M-y n-a-m-e i-s M-a-t-t-y."

"You ... you're the other ghost?" Charlie's voice was barely a whisper.

"I a-m."

I swallowed. "Do you know where the trick is?"

"Y-e-s."

"Will you show us?"

"I-f y-o-u h-e-l-p m-e."

I frowned. "Help you how?"

"S-e-t ... m-e ... f-r-e-e."

"But you're a *ghost*," said Charlie. "What do we know about setting ghosts free?"

"I think he means Mrs. Rothbottom."

"S-h-e h-a-s t-h-e p-o-w-e-r."

"Okay," I said. "If you show us where the trick is, we'll ask Mrs. Rothbottom to help you."

"P-r-o-m-i-s-e m-e."

Charlie and I looked at each other, then back at Matty. "We promise."

23

Matty floated ahead, leading us deeper and deeper into the yard.

"Do you trust him?" Charlie whispered. "He's got shifty eyes."

Matty swung around and shot straight at us. "I a-m t-r-u-s-t-w-o-r-t-h-y!"

"Sorry," squeaked Charlie.

Matty stared at us way too long. I was just about to grab Charlie and make a run for it when Matty turned back around and kept going.

We followed him, but I could tell Charlie wasn't happy about it. Neither was I. Maybe *Matty* was the one who was crazy.

We crunched through the snow. It was so cold I wished we'd grabbed our coats, but it was too late now. Besides, complaining gets you nowhere. That's what Dad always said. I wished he was here. He'd have taken care of us.

"Lacey?"

"Yeah?"

"Do you think he's taking us to the bog?"

"I don't know."

"I don't wanna go to no bog. You fall in a bog, you never get out."

"That's quicksand, not bog."

"Oh, yeah." We kept walking. "Is there quicksand in England?"

"I don't think on people's property."

"Good. That's good. But can we go back now? Please?"

"*No*, Charlie. We can't. We have to find the mojo bag. Just keep walking."

We did.

"Bogs aren't good." Charlie was talking to himself. "I can feel it in my bones, and my bones never lie."

After we'd gotten pretty far from the house, we started seeing things covered with burlap. They looked like a row of mummies wrapped in bandages.

"They're creeping me out," said Charlie, his teeth chattering.

"Me, too."

Suddenly, Charlie gasped really loud. "It moved! It's alive!"

"I-t-'s o-n-l-y t-h-e w-i-n-d, C-h-a-r-l-i-e." This time Matty's voice sounded kind. "T-h-e-y a-r-e b-u-s-h-e-s c-o-v-e-r-e-d f-o-r t-h-e w-i-n-t-e-r. T-h-e-y c-a-n-n-o-t h-u-r-t y-o-u."

I looked closer. Matty was right.

He started moving again.

"Matty?"

He stopped.

"Who wasn't telling the truth?"

"I s-w-o-r-e I w-o-u-l-d n-o-t t-e-l-l."

"Who made you swear?"

"I m-u-s-t k-e-e-p m-y w-o-r-d."

"Can you tell us how long you you've been here?"

"T-h-i-r-t-y - n-i-n-e y-e-a-r-s."

"You're kidding!" said Charlie. "You came looking for the treasure *thirty-nine* years ago?"

"T-h-e-r-e i-s n-o t-r-e-a-s-u-r-e." Matty's eyes looked really sad. "H-u-n-g-e-r c-a-n m-a-k-e y-o-u d-o f-o-o-l-i-s-h t-h-i-n-g-s."

I don't know why, exactly, but I blurted, "We're poor, too."

I knew it was true, but never, until this minute, had I said it out loud.

"T-h-e-n y-o-u u-n-d-e-r-s-t-a-n-d."

"We understand."

Matty moved past the bushes.

Charlie and I followed along behind, our feet sinking into the deep snow. I started thinking about the times Mom went to bed hungry so Charlie and I could eat. Everybody says money can't buy happiness, but they probably haven't gone hungry.

"Where's he taking us?" Charlie rubbed his arms really hard. "What could be out *this* far?"

"I'm not sure. But he knows where the trick is, and I trust him."

Finally, Matty stopped.

"Where are we, Matty?"

"I-n t-h-e c-o-r-n-f-i-e-l-d."

"Is the mojo bag here?"

Matty slowly raised his arm and pointed. "C-o-r-n-e-l-i-u-s w-a-l-k-e-d d-o-w-n t-h-i-s r-o-w."

As we moved in closer, Charlie and I could make out dried stalks. "Corn rows go on forever," I said. "Did you see where he put it?"

"T-h-i-s f-i-e-l-d d-o-e-s n-o-t b-e-l-o-n-g t-o t-h-e m-a-n-o-r. I c-a-n-n-o-t g-o a-n-y f-a-r-t-h-e-r."

Charlie looked at me. "That's what Daniel said, too, remember? That he had to stay at the manor, or in the car."

"C-o-r-n-e-l-i-u-s d-i-d n-o-t w-a-l-k f-a-r."

We headed down the row, the leaves scratching against our faces.

"I thought farmers cut down cornstalks before winter," Charlie grumbled.

The fog was so thick Charlie and I crouched down to see better. Long, shrivelled leaves lay all along the ground.

After about the twentieth stalk we started wondering if we were even in the right row.

"I don't see any bag." I pushed the snow off the leaves. It was so cold my hands went numb.

We kept looking, farther and farther. Charlie's breathing got really loud — it does that when he's upset. "It's *not* here, Lacey." He took a swipe at some dried-up corn.

"It *has* to be here. Matty saw him bring it out. It couldn't just disappear."

"Maybe an animal took it."

"There wasn't any food in the bag. Why would an animal take it?"

"I don't *know* why an animal would take it!" Charlie yelled. "I don't know why a *person* would take it! All I know is, without the scarf and the hair there's nothing to throw in the stupid river. I'm gonna be cursed forever!" He was really losing it. *"And I didn't do anything!"* Charlie kicked at a stalk. *"Why'd this have to happen to me?"*

He took off down the row.

"Where are you going?"

I went after him, but there was no way I could see in the fog.

"Charlie!"

I kept pushing my way past the cornstalks, trying not to fall on the uneven ground. "Charlie!"

My eye caught something fluttering near the ground. Something red.

"Charlie! I found it!"

I could hear Charlie running back.

"Over here, Charlie! Over here!"

When he appeared out of the fog, I held up the mojo bag.

Charlie yanked it out of my hand and opened it. "My scarf!"

As he pulled it out, something floated to the ground.

"Your picture from the family tree!"

Charlie grabbed the picture and stared at it for a long time.

"This is almost over, isn't it, Lacey?"

"I sure hope so."

He tucked everything back inside the mojo bag and pulled the drawstring.

We started back through the snow, feeling better than we'd felt in a long time. Then we heard a crackling sound.

Charlie whimpered.

More crackling, louder this time. And closer.

Charlie whispered, "Something's coming."

"Who's there?" I shouted.

That's when we saw it. A shape.

A long, black shape.

It hovered just above the ground, then slithered toward us like a snake. Charlie shook so hard he dropped the mojo bag.

The thing sprang forward, sucked up the bag and slithered back into the fog.

24

"L-a-c-e-y! C-h-a-r-l-i-e!"

It was Matty.

"F-o-l-l-o-w m-y v-o-i-c-e. Y-o-u-'l-l f-i-n-d y-o-u-r w-a-y o-u-t!"

Somehow I got my feet to move, and I pulled Charlie along to where Matty walked at the edge of the field.

"Something's out there," I said. "Something horrible."

"W-h-a-t d-i-d y-o-u s-e-e?"

I told him about the black shape that took the mojo bag.

"H-e-'s n-e-v-e-r d-o-n-e a-n-y-t-h-i-n-g l-i-k-e t-h-i-s."

"*Who* hasn't?"

He didn't answer, just said, "W-e m-u-s-t g-e-t C-h-a-r-l-i-e b-a-c-k t-o t-h-e h-o-u-s-e."

Matty led us through the fog. I made Charlie walk in front of me so I could keep my eye on him. As we passed by the bushes wrapped in burlap, I kept thinking, *Any second a hand's gonna reach out and grab me.*

Then one did.

"Matty!" I shrieked.

The burlap ripped and a body fell out, landing right at my feet.

I was staring at an old wrinkled face, the oldest face I'd ever seen. Charlie couldn't stop screaming.

Daniel suddenly appeared. "Get him inside!"

I grabbed Charlie. By the time I dragged him back to the manor he was beyond screaming. Now he was staring. Just staring.

I helped him into a chair, and Daniel wrapped a blanket around him.

"Can't you hypnotize him or something? Make him forget what he saw?"

"He's shut down. Hypnotism wouldn't take hold."

"We have to tell somebody about the body."

Daniel's face got hard. "No."

"No? Why not? Somebody *murdered* that old man!"

"No one murdered him, Lacey. He was already dead."

"*What?*"

"That's all I can say."

Daniel vanished.

"I'm calling the *police*!"

That brought him back fast.

"If the police come to investigate they'll see only you and Charlie here, and they'll take you away. They'd never leave two kids alone. And when you tell them Charlie has to sleep in water every night or he'll shrivel up and die, they'll put you both in an asylum. If that's what you want, call them."

I slumped down in a chair and put my head in my hands. This was all too much.

"**C-a-l-l M-r-s. R-o-t-h-b-o-t-t-o-m.**" Matty hovered in the doorway.

"Mrs. Rothbottom. Of course!" I looked around. "Where's the phone?"

Daniel shot to the far side of the Christmas room and pointed to a dark blue velvet curtain. "Look behind there."

I yanked it open. The phone was on the floor.

"What's it doing down there?"

"Cornelius couldn't risk you or Charlie calling for help."

I pulled Mrs. Rothbottom's number out of my pocket and dialed. It rang and rang. *Please pick up. Please pick up.* She didn't. When the answering machine clicked on, I left a message about finding the trick and the black shape that took it, then begged her to call as soon as she got home.

"*Robert's* got the trick?" Daniel asked before I even hung up the phone. I heard fear in his voice.

"How could that thing be *Robert*?" I asked. "He's in the attic! And he's a spirit!"

"Spirits can take many forms, Lacey. And they can move around at will."

We heard moaning.

"Daniel?"

"I hear it."

We slowly moved around the Christmas tree. Matty was staring into the fireplace. The sound was coming from inside the flames.

More moaning.

Both Daniel and Matty moved back. They looked scared.

"It's him, isn't it?" I asked.

Daniel nodded slowly.

When I saw how frightened Daniel and Matty looked, a rush of anger shot through my whole body and came out shouting. "This is all your fault, Robert!"

"Lacey, don't." Daniel's voice was weak.

"So *what* if you got betrayed? Thousands of people get betrayed every day! They don't put curses on people! Especially not *innocent* people. *What'd Charlie ever do to you?*"

The moaning got even louder.

Daniel moved closer to me. "He's angry."

"*He's* angry? Well, so am I!" I was shaking, but not from fear. I hated Robert — hated him for the suffering he caused Uncle Jonathan, and all the suffering he was causing Charlie and Daniel and Matty.

I leaned into the fireplace. "You want to be faced? Fine! *I'll* face you!"

"Lacey!" Daniel's voice turned cold. "That's not a good idea."

"*Why not?* I've got Darcy blood in me, too!"

"You don't understand. You may *die*."

"You and Matty didn't *know* what was up there. You were taken by surprise."

"Jonathan knew."

That stopped me — but not for long.

I started out of the room.

"You'll be sorry."

"L-e-t h-e-r g-o."

"Go back to your *chair*!"

I didn't turn around. "He smashed his chair, remember?"

"Do you know how many rooms there are in this house?" Daniel shouted. "How many *staircases*? You'll never find the right one!"

I walked out.

Matty whispered, "T-h-e r-o-u-n-d r-o-o-m."

25

Once inside the round room, I started climbing up the steps. The moaning sounded like it was right in front of me. I felt scared, really scared — but I kept going.

I passed the door in the wall, and I saw that it was open, but I knew it didn't lead to the attic. I had to go up. Attics are always up.

The moaning got even louder.

After about twenty steps it got so dark I could barely see. But I kept going.

"I'm coming to face you, Robert! I'm coming. Just like you wanted."

The moaning suddenly stopped, like someone had shut it off.

My mind started racing. Maybe it *wasn't* Robert. Maybe it was a tape recorder or something making a moaning sound.

"It's just a stupid trick!" I shouted. "Nobody's up there!" I bolted up the rest of the stairs.

As soon as my foot touched the top step, a wave of fear hit me. I could barely breathe, and my heart beat so fast I almost blacked out. I leaned against the wall to keep from falling. Sweat poured down my face — then a sharp pain stabbed my chest. I bent over, gasping.

That's when it hit me.

I was having a heart attack.

I don't know how, but I managed to stagger down the stairs and out of the round room. I stumbled over to the winding staircase and grabbed the railing. As Uncle Jonathan's eyes stared at me from his painting, the face of the dead man in the cornfield flashed in my mind.

I stopped cold.

"It ... it's *you*!"

"I wondered when you'd figure it out." Daniel slowly materialized beside me.

"That body in the field is Uncle Jonathan! But how? How *could* it be? He's been dead for a month!"

"No," Daniel said. "He died two days ago."

"Two days ago?"

"Less than an hour before you arrived."

"But the letter about the will —"

"That was to ensure your family would come."
I slid down onto a step.

"Jonathan wanted more than anything to personally explain about the curse and prepare Charlie for what was going to happen. He didn't make it."

I shook my head, trying to make sense of what I was hearing.

"Cornelius couldn't risk the ambulance being here when you arrived. There'd be too many questions."

"So he hid the body *outside*?"

Daniel nodded. "He knew the cold would preserve it. Heat does terrible things to dead bodies."

I looked up at Uncle Jonathan's portrait. His eyes looked so sad.

"Your uncle knew he was about to die and that the curse would pass on to the next male in the family. It tortured him because Charlie was an innocent child. Tortured him so much that even *after* he sent the invitation, he went up to the attic again. Only this time, he was too old and far too weak."

I could barely get the words out. "Something evil is up there."

"I know ... and so did he. But he wanted to protect Charlie — to save him from a life like his."

"When did he put that stuff about the curse in the bottle?"

"Minutes before he died. It's a trick bottle that repeats what's spoken into it. Charlie smashed it before he could hear everything Jonathan said."

The phone rang.

I raced down the stairs and into the Christmas room. "Hello! Hello! Mrs. Rothbottom?"

I told her everything, even about Jonathan's body in the cornfield and how I'd gone up to the attic to face Robert.

"You were foolish to go up there unprotected!"

"What else could I do!"

"Where's Cornelius?"

"In the village."

"Listen to me, Lacey. You and Charlie must get out of that house *immediately*."

"But —"

"Get out of there!"

I threw down the phone and ran to the kitchen.

Charlie was gone.

I raced back to the front entrance. "Charlie! Where *are* you?"

As I headed down to the arcade, Matty appeared right in front of me. I gasped and fell backward. *"U-p-s-t-a-i-r-s."*

I bolted back to the main floor and up the winding staircase. Charlie was on the landing, slashing Uncle Jonathan's painting with a knife.

"Stop it!" I grabbed his arm. "Stop it!"

"I don't want to be cursed anymore!"

"I know. I know."

Charlie pulled away from me and ran up to the second floor.

I followed him to Uncle Jonathan's room and watched in horror as his arm raised up over the water bed. "I'd rather be *dead* than have to sleep in this the rest of my life!"

"Noooo, Charlie!"

The knife came down hard. Over and over Charlie pierced the lining and the leather frame. As the water poured out, I wrestled the knife from his hand.

"I know how you feel, but —"

"You don't know how I feel! It's not happening to you!"

I flung the knife away. "Listen to me. We've *got* to get out of this house."

"And go where? There's *nowhere* to go!"

"Mrs. Rothbottom's waiting for us. She's figured something out. But we have to go *now*, before Cornelius —"

"Charlie? Lacey?"

"He's back," I whispered.

Then we heard the stairs creak.

26

"Charlie!" This time Cornelius's voice was sharp.

Charlie grabbed me. "He must have seen the painting! What's he gonna do when he sees the *bed*?"

"The window!"

We dashed over to it. There was only one latch, but no matter how hard I tried it wouldn't turn.

The stairs creaked some more. Cornelius's footsteps got closer. Then the doorknob turned.

The sound of sirens cut through the air. Flashing red lights were moving through the fog.

"*Police?* What are they doing here, Lacey?"

We heard the stairs creak again. Cornelius was heading downstairs.

"Mrs. Rothbottom must have called them," I said, "about the body in the cornfield." I didn't tell him it was Uncle Jonathan. "We were supposed to be gone by now. If they find us here, they'll take us, too!"

"Maybe Cornelius won't tell them we're here."

"We can't take that chance!"

Charlie paced back and forth wringing his hands. "If we sneak downstairs, they'll hear us for sure. This house creaks like crazy."

"We're not going downstairs." I tried to open the window again. "There's a balcony out here."

"And then what? We fly?"

"Think positive, Charlie."

"Yeah, sure. That always works."

I twisted the latch again, but it still wouldn't budge.

"Try this."

Charlie held out a brass poker from the fireplace. I banged the handle against the latch. Three hits and it turned.

Pushing through thick vines, we crawled out onto the balcony. It was way too far to jump, but pillars with vines growing around them went all the way down.

I turned to Charlie. "Remember *Jack and the Beanstalk*?"

"You're gonna *climb* down?"

"*We're* gonna climb down."

I swung my leg over the railing. "Come on."

He leaned forward, looked at the ground and shook his head. "I can't, Lacey."

"Yes you can!"

"Does this look like a body that can climb down pillars?"

"Hang on to the vines. They're thick. They'll hold you!"

"I'm too fat!"

"No you're not!"

"I can't, Lacey!"

The bedroom door crashed open. "They're getting away!" shouted a policeman.

When Charlie saw them, he practically flew over the railing. His chubby hands grabbed the vines and we started down. Don't ask me how, but he got to the bottom before I did.

As soon as our feet touched the ground we took off. Halfway down the driveway we heard a car.

"They're coming!" screamed Charlie.

"RUN!"

We ran as fast as we could, but the car caught up to us, spun around and stopped. It was a police car.

The window rolled down. "You're not going to get very far on foot," said Daniel.

A second later he was outside the car, holding the front door open. "The police are searching the cornfield. It won't take them long to find the body."

I jumped in the front seat and slid over.

"What are you doing, Lacey?" cried Charlie.

"Escaping! What do you think?"

"But ... but ... stealing a *police* car?"

"I shan't tell." Daniel smiled.

"Get *in*, Charlie! Hurry!"

Charlie got behind the wheel.

"Go to Mrs. Rothbottom," said Daniel. "She's your only hope."

"Come with us," pleaded Charlie.

"Can't leave, remember? Besides, I'd miss all the excitement." Daniel grinned and slammed the door. "Don't forget to write."

"What?" Charlie pushed his glasses up his nose.

"Just get this curse removed, and we'll all live happily ever after." He vanished.

Charlie jammed his foot on the gas pedal and we took off. At the end of the driveway he swung onto the road heading for the bridge. As we bounced over the wooden slats we spotted a car coming toward us.

"It's Mrs. Rothbottom!" I yelled. "Stop! Stop!"

Charlie slammed the breaks so hard we practically went through the windshield. Mrs. Rothbottom saw us and screeched to a stop.

When Charlie and I ran over to her she yelled, "What are you doing driving a police car!"

"It was the only way we could get away!" shouted Charlie. "The police tried to grab us!"

Mrs. Rothbottom motioned with her head. "Get in."

Charlie and I jumped into the front seat beside her.

"Are you two all right?"

"Yes," I said, "but I don't know what they're going to do to Cornelius."

"We can't worry about him right now."

As we headed toward the village, I looked back. All I could see was fog.

27

"Why'd you leave us this morning?" Charlie asked Mrs. Rothbottom.

"To get more ingredients for the curse removal. I told you I didn't have enough left for another attempt."

He looked relieved.

"Did you think I'd abandoned you?"

"Who, me? Nah. But Lacey was worried."

I elbowed him.

"I always finish what I start," said Mrs. Rothbottom.

I leaned forward. "But we don't have the trick. How can you remove the curse without it?"

"We go to Plan B."

Plan B? We waited for her to tell us. She didn't.

Mrs. Rothbottom turned off the main road, drove down a couple of village streets and stopped in front of a store called SOMETHING FOR EVERYONE.

"Since Robert's spirit has now become active," she said, "it's no longer merely a curse. And that's *extremely* dangerous."

Charlie's eyebrows went up. "That black thing was *Robert*?"

"I believe so." She shut off the engine. "Lacey, you said the curse on your uncle was placed by Robert on the day he was hanged."

"That's right."

Her eyes narrowed. "Curses cast just before a person dies are the strongest."

"Why?" asked Charlie.

"Because all the curser's vital energy goes into them." Mrs. Rothbottom leaned back. "The pieces are starting to fit. Your uncle moved to Hampton Hollow — the very village where Catherine Manridge lived. It makes perfect sense. He must have loved Catherine so deeply he followed her here. But because of the curse, he could only love her from afar."

She swung open the car door. "Let's go shopping."

Charlie looked at me. "*Shopping?*"

A bell over the door tinkled as we stepped inside the store.

We saw rows and rows of long tables filled with junk — the kind of stuff that didn't sell after a yard sale.

"So, what exactly are we were looking for?" asked Charlie.

"A doll, mirrors and some glue."

"You're kidding, right?"

"I never kid."

Charlie whispered, "She's gone bonkers."

"I heard that."

Charlie squinted. "What are we gonna do with a *doll*, Mrs. Rothbottom? Go ahead, tell me."

"You'll see."

We followed her down aisles so narrow we had to walk sideways. I kept knocking things off shelves and having to pick them up. Finally, Mrs. Rothbottom stopped at a table piled with dolls. Some were okay, but others had their arms or legs ripped off. One didn't even have a head.

Mrs. Rothbottom looked them over and then called out, "Mr. Hopkins."

A man with bushy gray hair came limping over. "What can I do for you today, Mrs. Rothbottom?"

"Would you happen to have a boy doll?"

"Not much call for boy dolls."

"Nevertheless, that's what I need."

Mr. Hopkins slid a cardboard box off a shelf over the table. It was filled with dolls, all shapes and colors. They looked like girls to me.

"Aha," he said, pulling out a doll wearing a sailor's suit. "Will this do?"

Mrs. Rothbottom smiled. "It will do nicely, Mr. Hopkins."

Next, we picked up two bottles of glue.

"And now, some mirrors," said Mrs. Rothbottom, heading for the other side of the store.

We looked around and finally found a stack in shiny black frames. "Now listen carefully, both of you. Don't look *into* the mirrors. Understood?"

We nodded.

She placed a handkerchief over the top one and told Charlie to lift the stack. Then she took three mirrors near the bottom and turned them over. When she handed them to Charlie she said, "Keep them upside down — and don't look!"

Back at the cottage we spread everything on the kitchen table — the mirrors facedown. Then Mrs. Rothbottom left. When she came back she was holding a hammer and a shoe box filled with cards and letters. She emptied the box into a wooden bowl and set it aside. "Plan B," she said.

Finally, we were going to hear it.

"Since we were unable to *remove* the curse that was cast on your uncle Jonathan and then passed on to you, Charlie, we're going to *reverse* it."

Charlie straightened his glasses. "Reverse it?"

"I know a very powerful spell that will send the curse, and all the negative energy attached to it, *back* to the person it came from."

"And all this stuff will do that?" I asked.

"It will, indeed."

Mrs. Rothbottom handed the hammer to Charlie. "Smash the mirrors. *Hard.*"

Charlie didn't ask why, just whacked the hammer against the back of each mirror. "Man, that felt good."

"Now spread the glue all over the inside of the box and press the back of the mirror pieces into it. Cover as much of the box as you can. Don't look into the mirror pieces — and don't cut yourselves. Not *one* drop of blood must be shed."

While we worked, Mrs. Rothbottom searched through her cupboards and took out some small brown bottles. When Charlie and I finished gluing on the mirrors, she undressed the doll and laid it inside the box.

"That looks like a tiny coffin," said Charlie.

"That's *exactly* what it is," she said. "Now, we need something that belonged to Robert."

"Where are we gonna find *that*?" whined Charlie. "He's been dead for seventy years."

"Women keep mementos."

"What women?"

"Catherine Manridge, of course."

"She's still alive?" I asked.

"No. However, her niece, Lavinia, is very much alive and well. With a little luck, we'll find that she has kept some of her aunt's belongings."

Charlie and I crossed our fingers while Mrs. Rothbottom made a phone call. Half an hour later the three of us were standing in front of a small stone house, knocking on Lavinia's door. We heard kids' voices, then a tired-looking lady wearing an apron answered. She was holding a baby. Four little girls stood around her, staring at us.

"Hello, Lavinia," said Mrs. Rothbottom. "These are the young people I spoke to you about."

"Yes, yes, please come in."

She pushed the girls ahead of her along the hall and told them to go and play quietly, then led us down some dark stairs. When she opened the door at the bottom, we stepped into a room filled with clothes piled up on old couches, chairs stacked to the ceiling, and tons of boxes, books and toys.

"It took a bit," said Lavinia, "but I did find a hatbox that belonged to my aunt. It has some of her things in it."

She passed the baby over to me and lifted a round, pale green box off a pile of Christmas decorations. She handed it to Mrs. Rothbottom. "There might be others. Look around all you like."

"It must have sounded pretty weird, us asking to see your aunt's stuff," I said.

She nodded. "I was a little surprised."

"Thanks for letting us come over," said Charlie.

Lavinia smiled. Her face didn't look so tired when she smiled.

"I haven't thought about Aunt Catherine in ages," she said. "After she died, Mum missed her so terribly she didn't want to live in their house alone. That's when she came to stay with us. When we cleared out her attic, we found this box."

172

It was probably rude, but I had to ask. "Did Catherine ever marry?"

Lavinia shook her head. "Robert was her only true love."

The baby started crying. I jiggled her up and down, but that made her wail even louder. "Odd you should come over today," said Lavinia, taking her back.

"Why is it odd?" asked Mrs. Rothbottom.

"Well, it's March 16. The day Robert was hanged."

28

There was a loud bang and someone started yelling. Lavinia rolled her eyes. "What I wouldn't give for a moment's peace. I'd best go sort this out. The girls will murder one another one day."

As soon as she left, Mrs. Rothbottom dumped out the green box. There were black-and-white pictures, letters tied with pink ribbon, and bunches of dried roses tucked inside plastic bags.

Most of the pictures were of Catherine when she was little — some with her parents, some with her sister. Finally, we found one of her grown up. She was standing next to a man with brown hair. They both looked happy.

"I wonder if this is Robert Collins?" said Mrs. Rothbottom. She turned the picture over. "Ahh, splendid." She showed us the writing on the back: *"Sunday in the park ... the day Robert proposed."*

She tucked the picture into her pocket.

"You're stealing it?" I whispered.

"Of course not. I'll ask Lavinia before we leave. If I remember."

"Look," said Charlie, holding up a book. "She kept a diary."

Mrs. Rothbottom grinned. "Read through it. There may be something useful."

"Like?"

"I have no idea."

"Then just how am I gonna know it's useful?"

She pointed a finger at him. "Start reading."

While Charlie read, I searched through the pile and found a mauve handkerchief with little roses stitched along the edges, a ring with a pearl in it, and some ribbons and letters. "What exactly are we looking for, Mrs. Rothbottom?"

"Something personal of Robert's."

"I don't think Catherine kept his hair or nails."

"Perhaps not, but we *must* find something to put in the mirror box or the curse cannot be reversed."

Mrs. Rothbottom and I searched carefully, but nothing looked like it belonged to a man.

"Hey!" Charlie sounded excited. "Listen to *this*."

Just as he was about to read, the door opened. One of the girls poked her head in, crossed her eyes and stuck her tongue out at us.

Lavinia appeared behind her. "Would you care for some tea? I'm making a fresh pot."

Mrs. Rothbottom smiled. "How lovely. Thank you."

The door closed again.

Her smiled faded. "What did you find, Charlie?"

"Friday, March 15. I visited Robert in jail for the final time. Neither of us could speak, our pain was so deep. I dried his tears with my rose handkerchief. Now these tears are all I have left of him."

＊

"Once we put Robert's picture and the hand-kerchief into the mirror box, we'll be set," said Mrs. Rothbottom as we drove home. "After dark we'll take the box to the graveyard and bury it."

"Why does everything have to happen *after* dark?" whined Charlie. "Can't we do something in daylight?"

"The veil between this world and the next is thinnest at night."

"What does *that* mean?"

"It means, my dear Charlie, that it's easier to accomplish things of a supernatural nature when human energy is low and spirit energy is high."

We both looked at her.

"*Spirit* energy?"

"I'll explain later. Don't want you worrying yourselves for nothing."

"Yeah, right." Charlie turned to me. "Like we're not gonna worry about spirits now that she's said it."

—

Back at the cottage we finished putting the mirror box together. Mrs. Rothbottom told Charlie to cut Robert's head out of the picture and glue it over the doll's face. When he was finished, Charlie held up the doll. "Creepy, eh?"

"Never mind that." Mrs. Rothbottom handed him the handkerchief. "Put the doll back in the box and tuck this beside it." She grabbed two brown bottles off the counter and slid them into her sweater pocket.

"What are those?" I asked.

"Red pepper powder and sulfur. Very powerful."

At ten-thirty we climbed into Mrs. Rothbottom's car. She told us the night watchman made his last rounds at ten, so he'd be home and in bed by the time we got to the graveyard.

We made a right turn off the road, and drove up a hill. At the top we saw a truck parked by the cemetery gates.

"He's still *here*," cried Charlie. "I knew something would go wrong. I could feel it in my bones, and my bones never lie."

I turned to Mrs. Rothbottom. "*Now* what do we do?"

She shut off the headlights and slowly drove the car behind some trees.

"We wait."

"For how long? Charlie's got to be in water by midnight."

"I seriously doubt Mr. Thatcher will stay until midnight."

"How do *you* know?" Charlie sounded worried. "He might stay all night. Who's gonna stop him?"

"Mrs. Thatcher for one. She'd twist his ears off."

We waited and waited.

Charlie kept checking his watch. "Let's just go to another cemetery."

"The nearest one is over an hour's drive," said Mrs. Rothbottom. "There's not enough time."

"So, we just *sit* here?"

"Precisely. And while we're waiting, I must tell you both something so you'll be ready for it."

"Uh-oh," I said under my breath.

"We may need help while we're in the cemetery."

"And just *who* is gonna help us?" asked Charlie.

"Spirits of the dead."

"Glad I asked." He put his head in his hands.

"The graveyard's full of them."

Charlie made a squawking sound.

"Actually, the world is full of them, but it's the ones in this graveyard that will assist us — *if* we need them."

I was so angry I shouted, "You said all we had to do was bury the box!"

"All we have to do *is* bury the box … and say a short incantation," she replied quietly.

I took a deep breath to calm down. "Then where do the spirits come in?"

"To make sure *Robert's* spirit does not interfere."

"Robert's in the attic! At Blaxston Manor!" I was losing it again.

"With any luck, that's precisely where he'll stay. However, there *is* a possibility, slight though it may be, that he'll attempt to stop the burial."

Charlie grabbed Mrs. Rothbottom's arm. "*How?* How will he try to stop it?"

"I'm not sure."

"That makes me feel much better."

"I may not know exactly *how*, but I do know that *if* he makes an appearance, his goal will be to prevent the box from being buried. *Our* goal is to make sure it *gets* buried ... and buried well. If I'm required to call upon spirits to assist us, I'm prepared to pay them."

I looked directly at her. "Pay them? With what?"

"Coins. I'll throw them over my shoulder as I request their help."

I shook my head. "What good is money to a spirit?"

"It's not the money, exactly. Balance is what they demand. Never take without giving."

"Look!" Charlie was pointing toward the cemetery.

We saw a flickering light moving through the gates. It was Mr. Thatcher's flashlight.

"Finally," said Mrs. Rothbottom.

Mr. Thatcher walked over to his truck and flung a sack into the back. Then he climbed in and started the motor. But instead of leaving, he drove *into* the cemetery.

29

"Where's the old fool going now?" snapped Mrs. Rothbottom. The red taillights on Mr. Thatcher's truck disappeared. "Charlie, get the shovel. We're not waiting a moment longer."

Charlie lifted the shovel out of the trunk, then we followed Mrs. Rothbottom and her flashlight as it moved over the ground.

"Where are we going to bury the box?" I asked when we got inside the cemetery.

"Someplace it won't be easily discovered."

She walked quickly along a winding dirt path. Suddenly she stopped, turned left and cut between the graves. The beam of light danced over the headstones.

Mrs. Rothbottom went pretty far in and headed down a steep hill. Then her foot slipped and she fell.

"You okay?" Charlie asked.

"Fine. Fine. No harm done."

We helped her up and she continued down to the bottom of the hill.

"These are the older graves," she said. "People rarely come here."

She stomped the snow with one foot.

"What's she doing?" I whispered to Charlie.

"I think she's dancing."

She moved down the row of headstones until she came to a really tall one. She stomped again. "Right here." She flashed the light in Charlie's face. "Start digging."

The ground was hard, but after a couple of tries the shovel sank in. Charlie dug a hole, piling dirt off to the side.

"That will do nicely," said Mrs. Rothbottom.

She took the brown bottles out of her pocket and got down on her knees. We crouched beside her.

"Take the lid off the box, Charlie — and don't look in the mirrors."

After he opened the box, Mrs. Rothbottom handed him the bottles and told him to empty both over the doll.

"Why can't you do this part?" he asked.

"*Your* energy must be on this throughout. Now sprinkle."

Starting at the head, where Robert's picture was, Charlie sprinkled the red pepper powder and sulfur over the doll's body.

When the bottles were empty, Mrs. Rothbottom closed her eyes, took three long breaths and let each one out with a soft whoosh of air.

"Here you are, Robert Collins, and here you shall stay. From this moment forward, all crossed conditions you have created, all curses you have cast, all evil thoughts you have or *will* have are sent back to you — just as these mirrors reflect your image back to you. And here, Robert Collins, you will stay, until you choose to release yourself to final judgment."

Her eyes sprang open.

"Close the lid. Now!"

Charlie threw down the bottles and slammed the lid on.

Mrs. Rothbottom handed him some rope and told him to tie it as tightly as he could.

He wrapped the rope around the box a couple of times and tied three knots.

"Do I bury it?"

"Yes."

Charlie put the box into the hole.

Mrs. Rothbottom closed her eyes again. "*May the curse that was placed on Jonathan Darcy go back whence it came, and may it remain forever with he who sent it.*"

She turned to Charlie. "Cover it."

Charlie pushed dirt over the box. When it was completely covered, Mrs. Rothbottom said slowly, "*What … was … done … is … now … undone.*"

Then she stood, raised her arms and looked up to the sky.

"*Let this dreadful deed reverse,*
And lift from all, this vicious curse.
As we stand in sacred space,
Return, oh spirit,
To your rightful place.
Grant forgiveness for what was done.
Dispense this spell with —"

Mrs. Rothbottom heard us gasp.

Then she saw it, too.

The box was pushing up through the dirt!

30

"Stop it!"

Charlie and I dove for the box.

Mrs. Rothbottom shouted, "Keep it closed!"

We held on as tight as we could, but the lid started to bulge. Something was trying to get out.

She ordered us to push the box back into the ground.

We tried, but it wouldn't stay down!

Mrs. Rothbottom made a strange movement with her hands and said in a loud voice, "I call upon the spirits of the night to assist us with this burial."

We heard a sound like paper crackling in a fire and then long, black shapes came straight up out of the graves and hovered above them.

Charlie screamed and fell backward. I tried to hold the box down, but it was too strong.

"Help us!" I begged.

The shapes didn't move.

Mrs. Rothbottom pulled coins out of her pocket. Just as she went to throw them, her body was yanked up in the air and flung backward like a rag doll. She hit a headstone with a loud thud and slumped forward.

"Mrs. Rothbottom!" cried Charlie.

I shrieked, "Hold the box, Charlie!"

"I'm afraid!"

"HOLD IT!"

Charlie grabbed it, and I leaped for the coins.

I wasn't fast enough.

The box exploded.

Everything in it shot up in the air and then came floating down in slow motion. The doll hit the ground and bounced three or four times before it fell back into the hole.

Out of the darkness, a deep voice said, "I await you."

The spirits raised their arms and sank back into their graves.

A voice cut through the air. "Who's there?"

Charlie and I whipped around and saw a yellowish light flickering in the darkness.

"Come on, Charlie!"

Charlie ran over to Mrs. Rothbottom and tried to lift her. "We can't just leave her here!"

"We *have* to! It's almost midnight!"

The light got closer.

"Charlie!"

Mrs. Rothbottom groaned, then her eyes opened a little. "Go," she whispered.

"Come on, Charlie! Mr. Thatcher's coming. He'll help her!"

I pulled him away. We raced through the graveyard until we found the road, and then ran along it to the gates.

Once we were in the car Charlie fumbled for the keys. He started the engine, drove in a big circle and headed down the hill. His whole body was shaking so hard his foot kept slipping off the gas pedal. The car jerked a lot but we made it down the hill to a fork in the road.

"Which way do I go!?" Charlie was yelling and crying at the same time.

I thought hard. "We turned *right* to go up the hill, so we need to go *left*. Turn left, Charlie! Left!"

Charlie made the turn, and in no time we saw lights in the distance. We got on the main road that wound through the village and headed for Blaxston Manor.

As we turned up the driveway we could see all the lights were off. Every one of them.

Charlie drove around to the back. When we tried the door, it was locked.

As I jiggled the handle Charlie looked at his watch. "It's twenty to twelve. How are we gonna get inside?"

I looked around, found a rock and threw it as hard as I could, smashing the window beside the door.

Daniel's head came through it. "All you had to do was knock."

"Robert showed up," I said. "He stopped us."

Daniel nodded. "I thought he might."

"Open up!" Charlie yelled. "I have to get in the bathtub!"

Daniel's head disappeared and then we heard the lock turn. The second we got inside we threw off our coats and bolted up the stairs. They were wet and slippery with water from Uncle Jonathan's bed.

"Where's Cornelius?" I asked.

"The police took him."

"But he didn't kill Uncle Jonathan!"

"They don't think he's a murderer, Lacey — they just need to find out what happpened. He'll be back soon."

When we got to the second floor we raced right past Uncle Jonathan's room to the bathroom down the hall. It had a really big tub. But when I turned on the faucet, a horrible sputtering sound came out.

I yelled and jumped back.

"What's *that*?" cried Charlie.

I knelt down again and tried to turn off the faucet but the handle just spun around and around. Then it started shaking like crazy. The noise got louder and louder, and suddenly the wall began to crack. Charlie and I backed up. The crack snaked up the wall, then water shot out.

Charlie lifted his arms to protect himself. "What's happening, Lacey!?"

"Use the bathroom downstairs!" shouted Daniel over the noise. "Hurry!"

Charlie and I raced down the stairs and crashed through the bathroom door.

As soon as we were inside, this bathroom started shaking so hard the sink pulled right out of the wall.

I turned the knobs on the tub. We heard the same loud sputtering and then the walls started to bulge. The bulge got bigger and bigger.

I knew what was happening. It was Robert. He wanted to be faced. And he wanted it to be tonight.

"I'm gonna die!" screamed Charlie. "I'm gonna die!"

31

I pushed Charlie into the hallway and slammed the door.

"There's another way," I said.

"Another way for what?"

"To break the curse. There's a second part to the curse I didn't tell you about."

"So tell me!" He was shaking so hard he could hardly stand up.

"Robert said, *'Every night of your life until you have the courage to face me, you must sleep in water or you shall shrivel up and die.'* That's the whole curse."

"*Face him?* How could Uncle Jonathan face him if Robert was dead?"

"Robert's spirit attached itself to Uncle Jonathan and followed him home."

"Home *here?*"

"Yes."

"And he's *still* waiting for Uncle Jonathan to face him?"

I shook my head. "Uncle Jonathan … is dead."

Charlie's eyes got huge. "He's waiting for *me* to face him?"

"I'm sorry, Charlie, but without water to sleep in, you're going to have to."

All the color drained from his face.

I called out, "Matty!"

In a second he was there.

"Tell us what happened when you went into the attic."

"N-o w-o-r-d-s c-a-n d-e-s-c-r-i-b-e t-h-e t-e-r-r-o-r I f-e-l-t."

"Find some!"

"I c-a-n-n-o-t."

"Then just tell us what you saw!"

"B-l-a-c-k-n-e-s-s. A-l-l w-a-s b-l-a-c-k-n-e-s-s."

"You don't die from blackness!" I screamed.

"I a-m a-f-r-a-i-d o-f t-h-e d-a-r-k."

"*Everybody's* afraid of the dark!"

Like a bolt of lightning, it hit me.

Everybody's afraid of the dark! Could that be it? Could that be what Robert wanted Uncle Jonathan to feel? *Fear?*

Daniel appeared beside Matty. "You have understood, Lacey."

"I'm right, aren't I? *That's* what Robert felt when they put the rope around his neck. *Fear.*"

"*Unimaginable* fear," said Daniel.

"Robert wanted Jonathan to feel what *he* was feeling."

Daniel nodded. "And that is why he put the curse ... on me."

"On *you*?

Daniel's ghost body started growing. Charlie and I stared in horror as it got taller and taller. His face got older, the lines deeper.

When the transformation was complete, we were looking at Uncle Jonathan.

"*What'd you do with Daniel?*" I shrieked.

Uncle Jonathan shook his head sadly. "There is no Daniel. I took the ghost form of a boy so you wouldn't be too frightened."

"*Why?*" squeaked Charlie. "Why did you take a ghost form?"

"When I died, my spirit would not pass on. I had not yet fulfilled my duty."

"You mean ... facing Robert?"

Uncle Jonathan nodded.

"He was an innocent man who suffered a most horrible death that he did not deserve."

"Then why'd you *do* it?" I asked. "Why'd you *lie* about him?"

"Jealousy is a vicious monster. I betrayed my best friend, taking not only his life but all that he loved. What I did was unforgivable." His head went down. "Unforgivable."

"You did a terrible thing to Robert, Uncle Jonathan. And now you're doing a terrible thing to *Charlie*."

There was such hurt in his eyes that I couldn't look at him.

"I have done *everything* in my power to help," he whispered. "I *truly* believed that the curse could be removed. I'm sorry. I'm sorry."

I grabbed Charlie's arm and pulled him down the hall. We could hear Uncle Jonathan crying.

32

"I can't face a spirit, Lacey!"

"You *have* to or you'll *die*. And I'm not going to let you die."

"If I *go* I'll die! Uncle Jonathan did! Matty did!"

"This time it'll be different."

"How? How will it be different?"

I stopped. "I'll be there."

Charlie swallowed hard. "You'll … you'll come *with* me?"

I nodded. "But first we need some candles."

"Candles? Why?"

I ran into the Christmas room. The carpet felt squishy under my feet. When I looked down I saw water all over the floor.

Charlie said, "Look!"

He was pointing at a radiator on the far wall. It looked like a black river was pouring out from under it.

"We gotta move fast," I said, racing over and

grabbing two candles off the mantel. "Matches, matches."

"Over there." Charlie grabbed a box from the fireplace. "What're we gonna do with the candles?"

"Remember what Matty said? The *darkness* terrified him. But if we bring *light* into the attic, we won't be so afraid. The darkness will be gone. See?"

"What's gonna stop Robert from killing us in the light?"

"We didn't do anything to Robert ... Uncle *Jonathan* did. *He* betrayed him, not us. He didn't have the courage to face his friend, but *we* can do it."

"Let's think this through. Maybe there's another way."

I looked over at the grandfather clock. It was five minutes to midnight.

"Sorry, Charlie. We've run out of time."

—◆—

Charlie and I tore up the winding staircase and along the hallway. When we got to the door leading into the round room we both stopped. I felt the hair on the back of my neck stand up.

"I'm scared, Lacey." Charlie's voice sounded far away.

"So am I."

We opened the door and went inside.

I groped around for the light switch, flicked it on, then showed Charlie the stairs.

"Staircase 13!"

Charlie turned to run but I grabbed him.

"We don't have any choice, Charlie. It's the only way to the attic."

"Thirteen's bad luck! *Everybody* knows that!"

"It's just a number!"

"It's thirteen! I'm *not* going up there!"

I shook him hard. "*Think*, Charlie. There's no water for you to sleep in tonight. You'll shrivel up and die!"

I must've gotten through to him because he calmed down a little and looked up the staircase.

"Are ... are you still coming with me?"

I nodded. "You're my brother."

He gave me a little smile and pulled the matches out of his pocket. First he lit his candle, then mine.

The higher we went, the more scared Charlie got. "I can't do this. I can't go up there."

"Yes you can, Charlie. You *can*."

The candle shook in his hand. "I hate this house. I *hate* it."

"We can go home tomorrow, I promise. Now keep going."

I had climbed about ten more steps before I realized Charlie wasn't beside me.

"What's *wrong*?"

Charlie's eyes looked crazed. "My legs won't move!"

I pounded back down.

"What do you *mean* they won't move!"

"I'm trying! Really, I'm trying!"

"They have to move! We don't have time for this, Charlie!"

"I know! I know! I can't help it!"

"Try harder!"

Charlie tried, but his legs were like lead. "I'm paralyzed! *Paralyzed!*"

He started crying.

"It's your *mind*, Charlie! Your legs are okay. I know they are!"

"Tell that to my legs!"

I looked at my watch. *"We only have one minute, Charlie!"*

"I'm gonna die!"

I tried with all my strength to pull him up, but he was frozen to the spot. "I don't know what to do, Charlie! I don't know what to do!"

"Get out of here, Lacey! Save yourself!"

"I'm not going!"

Charlie cried even louder.

Think. Think. There had to be a way to trick his mind. Then it hit me. "Ten times ten."

"What?"

"Ten times ten, Charlie. What is it?"

"Are you nuts?"

"What is it?"

"A *hundred*. So what?"

"Thirty-nine minus eleven."

Charlie frowned trying to think of the answer. "Twenty-eight."

"Forty-five plus nine."

"Um ... um ... fifty-three."

"Close."

As Charlie thought of the right answer I slid my hand under his arm.

"Fifty-four!"

"Right! Good one!"

His legs started moving.

"Eight times twelve."

I kept giving Charlie math questions to keep

his mind occupied — just like the *Brain Teaser* book did when we were on the plane.

We made it to the top, but Charlie was shaking so hard he dropped his candle. The flame went out as it bounced down the steps.

"Oh, nooo!"

"It's okay, Charlie! It's okay! I still have mine."

In front of us stood an old, cracked door with the paint almost completely peeled off. "We have to go in, Charlie. I'm right here with you."

I reached out, then pulled my hand back and wiped it on my sweater. I tried again. Curling my fingers around the knob, I turned it.

The grandfather clock started bonging really loud.

Charlie screamed, *"It's midnight!"*

33

"He's here!" I shouted, pushing him inside the attic.

Just as I went to step in behind him, the door slammed in my face. I pounded on it and tried turning the knob, but it wouldn't move.

I could hear Charlie screaming, *"Ahhhhhh! Ahhhhhhhh! Ahhhhhhhhhh!!"*

He was going out of his mind.

I pounded harder. The door crashed open and my candle lit up the room.

Charlie's eyes were shut tight, but his mouth kept screaming and the clock kept bonging.

Finally, it stopped. So did Charlie. He opened his eyes.

With hearts pounding, we waited ... and waited.

Nothing happened.

Shaking like crazy, Charlie looked around. "Where is he, Lacey?"

"I ... I don't know."

I took a few steps. There was an old rocking

horse, a chest, some lamps and lots of cobwebs
— but no Robert.

Nobody was here.

It was like the weight of the world suddenly
lifted from me and I started laughing.

"What are you *laughing* at?"

"You're okay, Charlie! You're *okay*! No heart
attack! No shrivelling up!"

"*What?*" Charlie looked at me like I was nuts.

"There's nothing *here*. There's *nothing* here."

Charlie took a couple of seconds to let it sink
in. "I've been scared out of my mind for *nothing*?"

"Yes!"

"Do you have any idea what I've been
through?"

I couldn't stop laughing.

"It's not *funny*, Lacey! It was horrible."

"I know!"

"Horrible!"

"I know!"

Charlie shook his head. "All I had to do was
show *up*?"

"Yes!"

He swallowed hard, then threw his arms
around me and whispered, "I'm not gonna die?"

I held him really tightly. That's when the
tears came. "You're not going to die."

A blast of freezing cold air shot into the room.

"Oh, no."

The room got darker and darker. Then a black circle formed in front of us.

"What is it, Lacey?"

Charlie was breathing hard and then I couldn't hear him anymore.

I suddenly felt wet and clammy. The room was cold, but sweat rolled down my back. Something was in the attic ... inside the blackness.

As the circle grew bigger, it started pulling us. The floor sank away and, without our feet even moving, the blackness sucked us into itself.

My candle went out.

"I ... can't breathe," gasped Charlie.

Neither could I. The pressure on my chest was so terrible I thought somebody was squeezing my heart.

I tried to fight it. I tried hard. But I couldn't.

I was going to die.

From somewhere deep inside, I heard myself say, "We ... know you were ... innocent ... Robert. ... It ... wasn't your ... fault." The pressure got worse. "You ... didn't ... kill ... that ... girl ... You ... didn't ... kill ... her."

Just when I thought my heart would burst, the pressure started to ease up a little. "You ... didn't ... deserve ... to die."

It eased up more. "You ... were ... innocent."

I felt a release and my body fell to the floor.

A small light appeared. It grew bigger and brighter, filling the room.

As I slowly looked around I saw shadowy shapes. "Charlie?"

He didn't answer.

I got up and took a few steps. The shapes got clearer and clearer.

We were still in a room but it wasn't the attic anymore.

A group of men dressed in old-fashioned clothes were standing around looking up. Who were they? What were they looking at?

I slowly turned.

An executioner stood on a gallows. Charlie was next to him.

"Charlie!"

He didn't move.

I ran over, but as soon as my foot hit the first step I was flung back onto the ground. I tried again. The same thing happened.

The group parted, and a man walked toward me, his hands tied behind his back. It was

Robert. He was being led by two policemen, and behind him was a priest.

They got closer and then walked right through me and climbed the wooden stairs. Robert took a couple of steps and stood where Charlie was — *exactly* where he was. Their bodies were together, one inside the other.

I raced to the front of the gallows.

"Charlie faced you! He *went* to the attic!"

Robert and Charlie stared straight ahead, terror in their eyes.

"Why are you doing this? *Charlie faced you!*"

The executioner reached for the hood, but Robert said, "No."

Then he looked out over the crowd. "I didn't kill the child! It wasn't me!"

Church bells started chiming.

Robert's body shook — so did Charlie's.

The executioner put the rope around Robert's neck.

"Please let Charlie go!" I begged. "He didn't do anything to you! It was Uncle Jonathan! Charlie didn't *do* anything!"

Robert's eyes burned into mine.

"You're cruel!" I shrieked. "Cruel and *evil*! You'll never be free, Robert! *Never!*"

The executioner pulled a pin out from the bottom of the lever.

"No!" I cried. *"No!"*

Then he wrapped both hands around it.

"NOOOO!"

"He's innocent!" A voice rang out behind me. I spun around.

"I lied! He's innocent!" It was Uncle Jonathan.

The executioner tightened his grip. He hadn't heard. No one had.

"He's telling the truth!" I screamed. "Robert didn't do it! Don't kill him! Don't —"

I suddenly realized my hands were *touching* the gallows! I didn't get pushed back!

I climbed up the slats just as the executioner slammed the handle down.

"NOOO!!!"

Somehow I grabbed Charlie's pant leg and pulled. His body separated from Robert's, and we both went flying off the platform. The trapdoors swung open and there was a sickening thud.

Everything went silent.

The only sound came from Uncle Jonathan. He was crying like his heart was broken.

Then, through the crying, we heard music. It was all around us.

Charlie's eyes were wide. What was he seeing? When I looked, the gallows was gone.

Robert was standing on the floor. He didn't have the rope around his neck, and his hands weren't tied.

A woman appeared next to him. Catherine.

Another shape formed. I cried and laughed — it was Matty. All three of them were smiling.

Uncle Jonathan walked slowly up to Robert, but when he reached him, his head went down.

In a kind voice, Robert said, "I forgive you."

Uncle Jonathan lifted his head and looked at his friend. Robert held out his hand, and Uncle Jonathan took it.

Sparkles appeared where their hands touched. The sparkles grew and grew until all of them were shimmering in pure white light. Then they vanished.

The music turned into the sound of wind, and the wind blew, swirling all around us. People started fading away. Darkness came.

Charlie squeezed my arm. "What happened?"

A piano started playing.

"Do you hear that, Charlie?"

"I'm not deaf."

Suddenly, the floor tilted and we went flying down a long chute. Screaming at the top of our lungs, we were finally spat out — right on top of a lady. All three of us crashed to the floor.

The next thing we knew, Cornelius was helping the lady up. He didn't seem to notice Charlie and me.

"Are you all right, Miss Briar?" he asked.

Miss *Briar*? I looked closer. The lady we landed on wore a dark suit and glasses, but she was definitely the lady who'd asked Mrs. Rothbottom for a love spell.

"I'm all right, Mr. Twickenham. But I believe I may have sprained my wrist."

Cornelius looked into her eyes. "Come with me, dear lady. I'll take good care of you."

Miss Briar smiled. "Oh, Mr. Twickenham, you're so kind."

"Please … call me Cornelius."

He helped Miss Briar out of the room.

"*Where* on *earth* did you two come from?"

"*Mom?*"

We scrambled up and peered over the top of a desk. Mom was standing with her hands on her hips.

"We didn't break anything," I said. "Honest."

"Well …" She gave a little laugh. "It wouldn't have mattered if you did."

Charlie and I looked at each other.

"It wouldn't?" we both said.

Charlie leaped up. "Why wouldn't it matter, Ma?"

Mom grinned from ear to ear. "Because Uncle Jonathan's lawyer, Miss Briar, just read me the will. You'll never *believe* what the dear soul left us."

"*What?*"

"His entire fortune!"

Charlie and I squealed, hugged each other and jumped up and down.

"And …"

We stopped jumping. Mom raised her arms up and threw her head back. "This *fabulous* house!"

Just then, a long crack raced across the ceiling and water gushed down all over her.